Ogundimu consistently produces visceral prose, and *The Longest Summer*, her most extended work to date, is her first masterpiece. The dinge of the Midwest and the despair of its inhabitants shine through, alongside a profound alienation. Humanity is reduced to a corporate script, while personal connections flounder under the weight of economic oppression, bigotry and surreal external forces. It feels like an environmental evil is persecuting the narrator, and its effects penetrate to the micro-personal level. A radical loneliness manifests as events unfold according to a logic that is not fate, but the result of human agency. The knowledge that other choices could have been made only exacerbates the sense of doom these circumstances elicit. Someone willed this hell into existence. A feel-good summer read.

— **Charlene Elsby**, author of *Hexis*

Every tightly written line of Alexandrine Ogundimu's accomplished debut novel sizzles with wit, dark humor, and humanity, seamlessly infused into a propulsive storyline that also slyly interrogates our Capitalist value-system. Protagonist and anti-hero Victor Adewale and the complex characters that surround him have much to tell us about class, race, sexuality, and above all soul-searching as a young person in the 21st century American Midwest.

— **Joanna Margaret**, author of The Bequest

Do you remember your early twenties? Think back. When every action carried weight, when friends were as important as blood? Alexandrine Ogundimu's The Longest Summer is beautifully alive with the flush of young adulthood. Victor Adewale and his friends felt totally real to me – lost, searching, bound by indecision, yet joyously alive – people I would have hung out with. If you buy just one book this summer, make sure it's this book.

—**James Nulick**, author of *Lazy Eyes*

With The Longest Summer, Ogundimu manages to tap into the very essence of what it means to be human in a world that literally ceases to have meaning... in the process, once again, proving to the world that she is one of the best at her craft. It is in the decayed city of Abboton, Indiana (an almost too-perfect portrayal of a very specific moment in time of a very specific part of the American Midwest) that a certain type of slow-motion violence occurs—quietly descending upon its denizens, and sending out never-ending waves of irreparable destruction. I mean... My father lays his rifle across the bed and tells my mother "One of us is going to die tonight." Holy Hell. Jesus Christ. WTGDF. This is one that is going to stay with you forever.

-Mike Kleine, author of **agbogbloshie**

# THE LONGEST SUMMER

## ALEXANDRINE OGUNDIMU

# CL◢SH

Copyright © 2023 by Alexandrine Ogundimu

Cover by Matthew Revert

matthewrevert.com

Troy, NY

CLASH Books

clashbooks.com

Publicity: Clashmediabooks@gmail.com

ISBN: 978-1955904735

*To Jason, Tasha, and Will. I forgive you.*

"I'm not a drug salesman. I'm a writer."

"What makes you think a writer isn't a drug salesman?"

— KURT VONNEGUT, *CAT'S CRADLE*

# MAY

# CHAPTER 1

My father Tunde is the only Nigerian, the only black man who belongs to this country club, which is why he insists on transacting his official or near-official business here: He must show that he is exceptional.

I have not been allowed here for five years. I am here now because I need his money. He chose this venue to intimidate me, remind me what I lost since I turned 18 and became the one thing he wasn't prepared to deal with: an American.

"I'll be very honest with you," he says. He's picking apart his Asian grilled chicken salad. The food here is the greatest hits of the Standard Indiana Menu, and it's revolting. Burger, salmon (obviously frozen), and Cajun pasta alfredo. Grilled chicken or shrimp (also frozen) for an additional $3.

It all tastes like blood to me. I'm sucking back what's in my nose, desperate not to leak from the shitty coke I did last night.

My phone silently rings in my jeans. I do not need to look to know who is calling. They've been calling me for weeks, making demands, as people often do when you owe them money.

He joined this place shortly after we moved to Abboton,

desperate for validation. Like every successful black man, he knows that financial prosperity can buy solace from racism if only you can buy your way into the right spaces, combine the accouterment of white nobility with the funk of blackness.

"I'll be very honest with you, Victor," my father continues. "I'm not going to leave you out in the cold. This would not be right. I made you a promise, when you were a baby and I was holding you in my arms, to take care of you. But I am not comfortable with your behavior and things will have to change." He shovels up some confettied lettuce. "I will, as always, open my wallet. For education, for career, for whatnot. But I'm not happy about it."

He will now enumerate my flaws. Some legitimate, others juvenile indiscretions committed before I had received my driver's license. He took a half day at work, something he can do as a Senior Program Director at Parker Pilgrim Pharmaceuticals, an essential redundancy within their organization, the only company keeping this city going in the aftermath of a mass exodus of Fortune 500 firms. What was once an up-and-coming Midwestern hub has degraded into a rusted out husk of depravity and horror, as people with time and without jobs find new and interesting ways to ruin their lives.

"Your mother has turned you against me, we know this. There have been mistakes on my part: I don't blame you entirely. That being said, you haven't respected me and you have been disruptive. I work very hard to support you and your mother and am not appreciated. You said I didn't deserve your respect, despite all I have done. I am used, endlessly."

I unstick my mouth. "I was 14." He looks up at me: mottled cheeks, black eyes over severe, elongated glasses.

"Excuse me?"

"When I said you didn't deserve my respect." I fight the amphetamine grind. How many tablets did I take again? Was it enough to get me through this, or just enough to take the edge off, or was it enough to fuck me up like I really wanted? "I was 14."

"It doesn't matter. No other son would say that to his father. None of these fathers have to deal with this from their sons." He holds up his stop hand. "I would appreciate if you didn't argue with me. I have suffered a great deal at the hands of you and your mother. Yes, suffered. Look around you. I have overcome so much, and would have gotten so much further if this ass hadn't been black. And you say I don't deserve your respect."

Through the windows you can see the golf course, somehow both burning and rotting in the late May weather. The lazy overpaid staff, made up mostly of the children and grandchildren of the membership, moves between greens completing tasks at their leisure as the land in their charge falls apart like everything else here. Fat white men in white golf carts cruise the hills like maggots. A banner reads *Men's Mid-Amateur Championship this Weekend sponsored by Parker Pilgrim.* Near us is Theodore "Teddy" Grynesburg III, absolute hellion, whose daddy still brings him around at least once a week for tennis and bean soup. Teddy just got back from a grip upstate on drug, vandalism and/or burglary charges related to robbing his own grandmother for cash and Oxycontin. One time I let him kiss me, an ill-advised and disgusting bit of mutual experimentation that made me feel weird enough that I never returned his calls. Teddy waves at us, and we wave back.

"Faggot," my father says under his breath.

My friend Lex texts to remind me to pick him up for the death metal show tonight.

"I'm sorry, dad. Honestly. I've had my own struggles. I mean, I'm still an Adewale. Still black."

"No, you are not. You cannot imagine what I have been through, coming to this country with no one, no mother, no father to support me, earning my degree, working to create this comfortable life that you waste and take for granted. What you have gone through is nothing. I have made sure of that your entire life. I raised you to be a decent young man, not a drunk or a faggot or whatever. And you have resisted this. You have been terrible to me. Some would say abusive. Yes, abusive, don't try to argue. But I have forgiven you, for my own health."

To take this from me. That is his great cruelty, to damn me to whiteness due to my mullato nature, as if the world doesn't see me for what I am, as though I haven't been called a nigger more times than I can count, as if I do not deserve to be held in the same space as him, as if any black American isn't mixed with something. He does this because my skin is pale brown and I shave my head for the sake of ambiguity, because I dress like a hardcore punk kid and listen to headbanging music.

"I'm trying to do better."

"Whatever. What do you need?"

"Security deposit, any broker's fees, and the moving van. I'll drive it there myself and leave the car. The subway can take care of me in New York. All the places I'm looking at are close to the university anyway. Also a per diem until I can find a job." My father loves any corporate or Latin phrase.

"Fine. Send me the documents. And when is it scheduled, your magnificent departure?"

"First week of August." I am infuriated and relieved.

"You are still working?"

"It's not going well."

He lifts his eyebrows. Like a real father.

"Somebody, we aren't sure who, took from the drawer."

"How much?"

When I opened the store after closing the night before and discovered the safe open, an entire deposit bag missing, $3,000 in cash, felony money, gone, and no idea who could have taken it, that was the moment I asked myself if this job was worth it, if the stress was enough to justify my meager wages that were still more than I'd earned in my life, and it occurs to me that this is a feeling my father cannot understand from his current upper-middle-class perch, if he ever could. "Enough. "

He looks at me over a 32-ounce golf ball-shaped beer mug. "Not you, I hope?"

*You fucker.* "Not me." My phone buzzes in my pocket and I know without looking that it's either Henshaw or Lex.

When I close my eyes I can see the Manhattan skyline. The rest of the summer stretches out before me, a vast field of long nights and shambling liquor stores, bummed smokes, pills crushed on the tanks of toilets. An even greater field is at my back, cresting in a wave, wind through Indiana corn, threatening to carry me under. The Midwest loves its children, but never wants to let them go. "I wish I could quit that job."

"No, you will not." He looks for a server. "I'm not paying for you to lay around. You're going to keep working. No job, no money. My job is awful too, Victor. My job is miserable. *I* am miserable. If you quit that job you're not getting one scintilla from me. Let me make this very clear: If you come and tell me there you've lost your job, if I hear about any of your silly drinking, if there's any trouble involving 3:00 AM calls, if you show any signs of misbehavior, of the old Victor, you can expect no further help from me."

The Adderall I needed to get through this meeting was chased with the Evan Williams stashed in my trunk. My coping methods for this unforgiving mushroom city and the associations I have made along the way are my business, not his. I have a flashback to surreptitiously sharing a joint with a shaggy-haired boy on the 16th hole on my 16th birthday. We had thought this fitting.

My phone rings again. The number is unmistakably that of a collections agency.

# CHAPTER 2

When Lex and I arrive at Henshaw's house in a blaze of pop-punk and enough whiskey scent to justify a field sobriety test I call his cell phone, the appropriate way to announce your presence. Only the rude and ignorant knock on people's doors.

No answer. Call again. No answer. Swear loudly, call again.

I get out of my car and bound up the three concrete steps onto his porch, knocking loudly. I've shed my pale blue dress shirt and am now clad in the band tee I had on under it.

"Hey wait," Lex says. He slams my car door and runs up behind me. I picked him up from his under-the-table job at a fast-casual/butcher shop restaurant concept. Abboton is a test market, where brands flock to in order to try out new and disgusting products on the soft, bored masses.

Demographically the city is similar to the United States circa 1980, with a large and very poor black minority and even larger white majority. There's a rapidly shrinking middle-class due to the economic downturn that has turned much of the Midwest into a hellscape of open strip mines and plastic factories. It's the ideal place to try and make the leap from trendy, wealthy, white urban youth to subdivision dwellers.

I knock, four times, hard and loud. A cop's knock, so that I'll get the response I desperately need. Henshaw is an ex-Marine who demands punctuality and respects cops.

A light brown, very skinny young man in red briefs opens the door, holding an unlit cigarette. "Are you the police?"

"Dude, put some pants on," Lex says, shielding his eyes as though he may become vicariously gay through looking at a mostly naked man.

"Hey Kyle," I say. I brush past him and into the living room of mismatched furniture. Lex won't cross the threshold. "Is Henshaw here?"

"Oh no, it's just my manager," Kyle says. He sounds bored, like he always does. "It might as well be the police, though. Have you come to chew me out off the clock?"

"I'm looking for Henshaw. I don't even chew you out that much."

"My roommate hasn't graced us with his presence." Kyle languidly strolls in and flops onto a couch. He reaches out and grabs one of a handful of orange bottles on the glass coffee table. "Pill?"

"Yeah. Wait no, what is it?"

"Dresdenol. Blue Disaster." He pops one in his mouth and throws me the bottle.

I hold it to the light, peer inside at the small, round, medium blue tablets stamped with *PP 100mg*. "Never heard of it."

"Melange. Dolls. Harris. Firebombs. It makes time solid. It liberates you from linear 3D space. It is phenomenally good shit."

"Firebombs?" The label says *Parker Pilgrim Pilot Program*.

"So called due to the similarity between the brand-name and the fire-bombing of Dresden during World War II."

"Gross." I toss the bottle back. He doesn't catch it, but lets it bounce off his chest then land in his crotch. "Thought you took Adderall. What do you need painkillers for?"

He waves behind him and pulls his phone out of a couch cushion. "Back pain. He's probably going to meet you there."

"Yeah, back pain," Lex says. "Alright, I'm going to change." He ducks into the hall towards the bathroom.

"Oh, by the way," Kyle says. "Our fearless leader wants a word with you."

Okay, so Kyle. This one is complicated.

Kyle is the kind of person who wakes up every day one step closer to suicide. He thinks it's because of his parents, the town thinks it's because he's a homosexual, but I think it's because of the town.

Kyle is my junior sales associate. A former college classmate and kind of friend. We had History of the Methodist Church 201 together and started hanging out. I'd buy him beer and help him study. I think he had a crush on me. But once he came around my buddies, Lex and Henshaw and the other townie fucks I've collected over the years, a veritable cavalcade of aggressively heterosexual bros, he soon understood that I was straight and dropped his (admittedly flagging) interest. He's a bright kid.

Then he dropped out his first semester of sophomore year, when I was trying to stay sober enough to corral grad school applications. I didn't really see him much after that. Some said it was due to addiction problems, but I chalked it up to economic pressures of working his way through private liberal arts college.

So when he called me up almost a year ago, saying he needed a job, I thought the least I could do was bring him on. I conducted the interview, totally softballed all the questions. He's fine at his job, considering it's just hanging up shirts. My eyes trace down his body and linger around the outline of his dick. He's put on weight which smooths out his jagged features, and he's finally learned to cut and dye his hair. Being in the same room with him like this creates uncomfortable feelings of ownership.

His dad kicked him out on account of him being everything that he is. All he does is watch makeup tutorials. The guy that owns this place, Henshaw, he took out a mortgage he couldn't afford, after the housing market had already rebounded from the recession. I hooked the two of them up. Fate, as it does, provided. I feel like he is my responsibility, and that any friction at work or home should be smoothed over by yours truly, lest the stress crack him in twain and he fulfills his destiny with a rope and a chair.

"Do you want to come with us?" I ask.

"Thanks to you I work seven days in a row. 4 hour shifts too. Thank you so much, V."

"Don't call me that. I know, I'm a real hell of a guy to just give you a job."

Erica texts me a selfie. It's a high angle, and I can see all the way down her blouse. I drove her to the clinic in Bloomington a few months ago, and paid for half of it. Maxed out one of my dwindling cards to do it. We weren't sure if it was mine or not, but thought it best not to tell Shaw either way. He'd be able to tell when it came out, by the texture of the hair, the shade of the soft baby flesh. I thought it wise not to test the limits of his good will.

"Who's that?" Kyle asks.

"Erica," I say without thinking.

"You shouldn't be fucking Shaw's girl. He'll kill you. He's killed for less. I have a friend for you, if you're so desperate for company. A very attractive, worldly person, stunningly androgynous, sharp sense of humor, absolutely dying to meet you since observing you through a store window. You had flowers in your hair."

"I don't wear flowers. Guy or girl?"

"You used to wear flowers. Back when I met you." He looks up from his phone. "Which would you prefer?"

"I'm not gay. Why do you all think I'm gay?"

He shakes his head and ignores me, stares back down at the phone. The pills are definitely having a soporific effect. How long has he been taking those things? There's a ripple of irritation at his flaccid lie. He doesn't have chronic pain nor any injuries. He's just taking them because they make him feel good, which I wouldn't begrudge him at all. My illegally obtained Adderalls help me focus and make me productive. It's a minor betrayal that he won't just level with me.

Lex wanders out of the bathroom wearing a tall tee with And 1 sneakers plus jean shorts. "Ready to go," he says.

"Wait," Kyle says. "I wanna go with you."

"Hurry the fuck up," I say.

He stumbles into his room, which I know from experience is a pigsty with a mattress on the floor. I hear crashing and swearing as I check the time on my phone. It rings and I pick it up.

"You on your way?" Henshaw's voice is a coarse tenor. I can hear the noise of the crowd. "This place is packed. Get your ass down here. Are you listening to me? Hey? Hello?"

# CHAPTER 3

"You need to stop calling me."

"Hello Mr. Adewale. I'm calling from Solutions International in regards to your account."

"I know why you're calling me, and I know you know that I can't pay you a goddamn thing. So why don't you quit calling. Or maybe if you'd rather you can come down here and get your pound of flesh from me in person."

"Sir, that will not be necessary."

Happiness is having a pitcher of Amber Bock all to yourself.

"I'm with my friends. I'm at a show in the middle of the night, and you're calling me."

"Your total debt is now in the amount of $12,582 and if we cannot receive payment we will be forced to take other measures."

"Do you know that minimum wage in Indiana is $7.25? I make ten bucks an hour. You're more than welcome to take my entire goddamn paycheck."

I hang up. Kyle sits next to me on the picnic table in the backyard of Sticks, inexpertly and not all that surreptitiously rolling a joint. He's not drinking on account of the pain pills.

I'm drinking for two, which amounts to me drinking exactly as much as I do anyway.

"What did you say about Britt earlier?" I ask.

He looks at me with those eyes that know too much. "You really want to talk about our boss now?"

"Not really."

"Collection calls are always a bummer."

"It's not any business of yours."

"God forbid I show any concern." He returns to the joint. Licks it shut and lights it. "If I had to guess," he says slowly. "Britt wants to talk about all that missing cash."

"I don't know what you're talking about. And if I did, regulations prevent me from speaking about it."

"Yes, V. Don't talk about how we got robbed. Just smoke weed with your subordinates. That's what a good manager would do." He takes a drag and holds it out to me. "How much do you owe the bank?"

"Don't call me V. I'm not smoking weed with my subordinates. Am I?"

He giggles without humor. "Would, let's say, three grand help you in your bit of trouble?"

The joint is tightly wrapped but on the thin side. I shake my head. I don't really smoke weed. Brings things too far into focus without sharpening me up. Last thing I need is to take a good look at myself.

He shrugs and takes another hit. "What I'm saying to you, V, if you'd listen for once, is that it's Thunderdome time. Heads are gonna roll. I've seen this happen before. My mother worked Loss Prevention at Macy's."

"May she rest in peace."

"Most of the loss came out of employees. That's where they're going to look, my captain. And given that you're by far my favorite manager and I do not want any more meathead, edgy, video gaming bros in my life..."

"How are things with Henshaw?"

"...or perhaps worse, another preening skank, I'd rather

you kept your job." He takes another pull. "The sooner you conclude that it was a rounding error, or stick it on some other associate, or lock arms and say hang us all or none at all, the sooner you and I can live and die in peace. To answer your question, Henshaw is an excellent roommate and any rumors of tension between us are fabricated."

"I've heard no rumors."

"Silly me. I must have been speaking to myself in the mirror again. It happens when I disassociate. The future runs backwards."

"You two making out over there?" says a coarse, masculine tenor from across the patio.

Lex trails Henshaw by a few steps, each clutching their own $5 pitcher of Amber Bock. You can't walk next to this guy on account of how much space he takes up. Henshaw, the big meat wall. Half his muscle's gone to fat, but the gym, then the Marines turned him into such a beefy killing machine that gaining weight has only made him scarier.

I don't remember how we met. All I know is that one day I came out of a haze of painkillers and alcohol to find myself eating a very late brunch at a Denny's with him and Lex, and the three of us have been running buddies ever since.

Henshaw doesn't say why he was discharged, and none of us have been able to discover why. It could have been any number of things based on his current behavior. Addiction, verbal abuse, insubordination, fighting, sexual harassment, sexual assault, money laundering.

Right now he's on the phone, talking half to us and someone else, speaking almost entirely in monosyllables.

"Right. Bye." He hangs up. "Anyway. Glad to see you managed to show your faces. About time you got this one out of the house."

"Everything still good with you two?" I ask.

"Couldn't be better." He rubs his white, freckled left arm. The motion makes his too-small Parker Pilgrim 5k Fun Run t-shirt ride up his arms. "I play Xbox, he stays in his room all night. Barely eats anything, too. It's perfect."

Kyle finishes the joint. "I am literally dwelling in Elysium."

"See."

"Elysium is in hell," Kyle says.

"Who were you talking to on the phone?" I ask.

Henshaw taps the side of his nose and winks at me. "Trying to make a little extra cash. A lot of irons in the fire. Afraid I can't share much more. Nondisclosure agreements are a real bitch."

There is a tacit agreement among all four of us to ignore Henshaw's drug dealing. He conducts business without us, and very infrequently.

"You gotta keep your hustle on," Lex says. "My man here knows that."

When around Henshaw he reverts to a hype-man, side-kick kind of wincing second-string attitude. It's pathetic. My understanding is that Henshaw defended Lex in high school from bullies, who didn't take kindly to the mildly autistic white rapper. The idea of Henshaw as anything but a bully is in itself laughable.

"See? Even Lex here gets it," Henshaw says. "Game never ends." He's eyeing this blonde woman in a Metallica tank, way out of his league even though she's like 40 and thus way older, the kind of old girl rocker you see everywhere in Indiana. You just do not try to hook up at a metal show, it's not done, but Henshaw's tried at every kind of show we've gone to, because he's a complete sex hound, endlessly hitting on and collecting women. He'll string a bunch of them along at a time, not telling them about each other, playing dumb when he's inevitably caught. His latest is Erica, who has broken up with him but still maintains an occasional sexual relationship. I'm unsure why. He's shockingly ugly, with a big head like a baby and a pug all mixed up.

Thinking of Erica, I check my phone. She's texted me.

*You coming over later?*

"Who are you texting?" Henshaw asks me.

"No one."

Kyle looks at me sideways but I ignore him, impressed with my own ability to be cool. I'm sure Henshaw wouldn't kill me. I just don't know how angry he would get.

"Girl, I bet. Trying to get some pussy for once in your life. About goddamn time too. I thought black guys were way better with the ladies, but boy, you've been proving me wrong. Oh don't look like that, I'm messing with you. We're all friends right? We're all friends here. Game never ends."

# CHAPTER 4

The set finally begins: the familiar ethereal/orchestral intro winding you up, then the preliminary drum fill and chugging guitar battering you back down, that moment makes you alive. Kyle has elected to stay outside and smoke more, but the rest of us are here with bared teeth, unable to suppress the savage desire animating us.

The real band, Voiding Emesis, bursts with an intensity openers can never match. Notes flying off downtuned fretboards, backed by machine gun drums, the vocalist's roar guttering into the crowd. They are angry with us but we're angry with them. All of us are angrier at something else, different for each but really the same: that world outside the bar.

The too big crowd packed before a low stage with no barrier between us and the band, we hit and hurt. Each of us an individual: "tank-top guy," "beard guy," "unbelievably huge guy," but really a congregation and a mob. This is a ritual. Who cares if the band is sloppy or the mix is shit? What matters is the energizing push of making us bang our heads together until we bleed. The beat drops and the mosh pit opens up.

I glimpse Henshaw standing at the back, too old and cranky for the pit. He's talking up the blonde.

Lex makes a point of pushing me. He's pogoing around like it's fucking 1998. Limbs swing, elbows slam soft flesh, wet hands slide on drenched shoulders. Somebody falls and three of us grab him and throw him into another guy, laughing. The floors are a slick flypaper of spilled beer and soda. The guys in front brace themselves against the stage so the heaving wave of humanity won't flow into the band and mess up the music. Lex's mass flies around, knocking everyone aside, met only by shorter guys who hit low and hard. I smile and scream and feel, finally, myself. No job, no father. No me.

I give Lex a fat elbow. It sends him reeling, laughing.

This is why I was in such a hurry. Here is what I live for: bodies flying, flesh smacking flesh, ritual dissolution of anger into sweat and music. The sacred rite of scrapes and bruises.

I check my phone after I catch my breath. I'm hanging off to the one side with the girlfriends and old timers who come to nod along.

Erica's texted me again. *You should see what I'm wearing,* she says. *It's blue.*

When the band hits a long solo the vocalist drops the mic and throws himself on the crowd. We bear him up, hands above our heads in tribute. He's one of those thin, long-limbed dudes, resting on his back being passed from hand to hand. He reaches up and walks himself spider-like, across those low, low ceilings, as we roar our approval.

We are all wet with each other's sweat and our faces are darkened in the low red light. My face connects with the back of someone's head and my lip tears. The vocalist hauls himself back onstage, as the lights strobe and we all push each other, skin on skin, and I'm alive I'm finally fucking *alive* again after months of dull nonspecific unease. And who cares that my name is *Victor* not *Vic* and I hope they can hear us in heaven. And I want to run into the night and *fuck* and *fight* and *let go go go.*

In between songs I can see Erica has sent me a picture. She is wearing blue – a sheer top I can see nipples through and her lips are in a fake down-turned pout. The teddy is the same color as her hair.

*You make me feel silly for wanting you so bad.*

The wave of the pit catches me again and I'm sent skidding to the other side of the room. I feel a moment of dread for the glass screen of my phone, but it's fine.

# CHAPTER 5

I'm finishing my fourth pitcher on the trunk of my car. My tongue pokes at the almost-bleeding upper lip. The air is still warm with the long-burned gasoline smell and the little crunching gravel echoes of people finding their cars. Kyle is waiting for me in the car, listening to Enya.

"What are you going to do about it?" Henshaw asks. The blonde is scooching between Henshaw and her baldhead fiancé, but they're pushing each other anyway. Henshaw is the taller and broader, the other guy firmer, smaller with a lower center of gravity.

I know how this will end. Henshaw's fucked for gas money. One time, he banged one of his exes in a hotel room and just left her there to pay for it. Her husband was pissed, but luckily the couple live in Louisville.

Henshaw's slept with every one of my exes. He's gotten slapped countless times, been engaged twice, fired for sexual harassment. And as you know, never speaks about his troublingly brief stint in the military.

What I mean is, any goodwill he has toward women comes off false. With every fuckup it becomes harder and harder to believe that he just has bad luck or picks wrong. You start to know it's him.

This doesn't get talked about because this notion would never fly in bro circles.

But as I sit on the car, hollow pitcher in my hand, I am looking at my own list of explosively failed relationships, each with their own accompanying resentment. And the sense that maybe something is wrong with me too expands. It slobbers at my ears when I look at one of the few women my age in the bar and wonder what the color and cut of her panties are like.

The guy takes a swing at Henshaw. And Henshaw, the big meat wall, he blocks the arm and puts the guy into a head-lock, and you can tell he's whispering in the guy's ear, telling him to back the fuck off, before he gets actually hurt. He has reverted to his military ways. I can see his body language change, become hungry, bloody. The blonde and Lex try to break them up: Lex not wanting his boy to go to jail, the blonde not wanting her man hurt.

I dismount the trunk and leave the pitcher standing on the parking lot gravel, as I get in the car.

"We ready to go?" Kyle asks. He looks ready to sleep. "Have you completed your savagery?"

I point at the knot of Henshaw and his adversary.

"Jesus. Can you take me home? I'm tired and literally cannot stay here any longer."

The thought of fucking Erica while her boyfriend/ex-boyfriend wrestles a drunken biker in a dive bar parking lot fills me with perverse joy. I feel my dick harden just a bit as I throw the car in gear.

Does this make me a bad friend? I don't know. Do I care?

# CHAPTER 6

Erica and I smoke on the balcony of her apartment.

"I shouldn't, but fuck it." She lights and exhales, flipping her shoulder-length sideways-parted hair. "So Shaw ditched you."

"I ditched Henshaw."

"Oh damn."

There are new spots of pain: sucked-out hickeys that hurt where my shirt brushes against them, and the nail marks Erica loves to inflict. The bruises have a duller, deeper, but no-less-satisfying hurt. My hearing is still fuzzy and what a more charitable person might call thoughts in my head are mostly sighs, thumps, and growls. I shiver with pleasure in the inky night air.

"We didn't wake your roommate up, right?" I ask.

"She's out. Why do you think I wanted you to come over? I get to be as loud as I want, for once. Did he leave you for a girl?"

"Do I have to answer?"

"You always get so mad when he abandons you." Erica says. She punches me on the arm. Everything, everyone in Abboton is hitting me. "It's whatever. Not like I expected him to stop whoring around. One girl to the next. Always says he cares, never does. "

"You're so judgmental. How am I not a whore?"

She smiles. "You're my whore, baby. You're my favorite booty call." She looks down at her feet, then away from me and across the quiet complex. "Honestly, I'm mad I had to send you pictures. I shouldn't have to work that hard."

There is no reason for me to be attracted to Erica. She's weird-shaped. Bottom heavy with stubby legs. Her accent is a little trashy and annoying, her job is even shittier than mine — she always smells like fry grease — she has no education and manners, wears an ugly eyebrow ring, and her Manic Panic electric blue hair looks cheap and shitty. I hate her tattoo, and her taste in music sucks. But I love being here, and every time I see her I want to bury my face between her legs.

"Why do you hang around me, anyway?" I ask.

She leans over the balcony. "I don't know. I got no reason to. You're kind of mean, I want a relationship, you don't. Like I don't even know why. You're half-black and that would drive my mom nuts." She smokes in silence for a while. "Do you want me to be honest? You reliably put out. Don't make more of this than you should."

"I am thinking," I say, attempting to craft something through the lingering fog of Amber Bock, "That it would be best if we didn't do this anymore. It's kind of shameful to run around like this. I'm not getting what I want out of us hooking up. And, hang on a second. I don't know what I want, but this ain't it."

She leans her body against mine. I grab her right butt cheek and pull her close. She purrs a bit and I kiss her, not too hard.

She pushes back with tongue. Erica's not a very good kisser, but she's enthusiastic. My mouth is very wet. As she pulls away she bites the swelling on my lip.

"Your body says otherwise," she says. "You ought to listen to it."

"I think this is the last time. Besides, Kyle seems to think that Shaw is about to take my head off over it."

"Oh of course, Kyle. Can't think of no other reason why he might not want us to hook up."

"Kyle and I have never so much as kissed. I'm not gay."

"Whatever, cake-eater. I gotta pee."

She wraps her robe tighter as she heads inside, leaving me in unbelted pants and no shoes to blow smoke rings at the moon. Somewhere in the complex a girl shrieks and then laughs, and country music floats around.

# CHAPTER 7

Parker Pilgrim Pharmaceuticals, America's 12th largest drug manufacturer, was founded in 1890. Originally based in Chicago, they moved to Abboton on account of being too small to afford to pay off the local government to look the other way at their blatantly illegal experiments. The First Families of Abboton, the true power behind the city, they saw fit to invite them down, make them feel at home, offer them an indecent tax break and an entire population of test subjects only too willing to make and consume their substances.

As of now they are the largest remaining manufacturer in the city, employing about 5% of the population. Through an agreement with local clinical testing centers they employ many more as temporary guinea pigs.

In 2018 Amory will find these notes and she tells me they sound right, almost exactly as she remembers what we now call "the longest summer." She has gotten to the end of this sentence and has called to ask if it's really true, if I could predict events with this much clarity when I wrote all this. I'll tell her that I can, but only if they aren't important.

Despite mostly producing generics, they have been looking for a breakout hit. Their latest and arguably greatest is

Dresdenol, a synthetic painkiller they falsely claim is less addictive than Oxycontin or Vicodin. Street name is Blue Disaster, so named for both the color of the pill (Dresden Blue) and the hallucinogenic properties brought on by overuse, which can lead to bad trips. Side effects include constipation, impotence, and a disconnection from time and space itself, as you experience possible pasts and futures in tandem with your concurrent reality, sending the user into a semi-prescient fugue state where all possible moments are experienced simultaneously as a 4D hyper-structure.

I am standing in Henshaw's living room, looking at the bottle of pills in 2012. I will learn about Dresdenol from a clinic doctor a year from now. But since I know it then I know it now, even though I am yet to fall so deeply into my own mental illnesses as a result of my continued failure as a son that I begin to take Dresdenol recreationally. The now of that longest summer is not the now of my recollection, nor is it the now of my infinitely fractured and prismatic future. I am here and there at once, and now you are too.

# CHAPTER 8

"Hey guys, welcome to Redacted. Anything I can help you find?"

Britt takes off her Wayfarers. "Guys?"

I clench. "Sorry. Wasn't paying attention."

"Obviously. Have the ACES been wild?"

I'm trying to straighten the Music t-shirt wall. "Hard to see sometimes. What did you say?"

"Any shoplifters?"

"Not that I know of."

"What do you know? And what happened to your face?"

She bumps around in back for a minute and I tense up, then relax and force myself to remember that Britt always says she wouldn't come in on her day off to fire someone.

My head and ears are still fuzzy and pounding from last night. Sandy, the only other Host besides me and Britt who knows what they're doing, carries an armload of Aquaman shirts to SuperHeroes And Miscellaneous Brands, a.k.a the SHAM wall. The stack goes over her butch little head.

The in-store Internet radio we aren't allowed to change starts playing "Thrash Unreal" by Against Me!, and I sing along under my breath without meaning to.

Two swole guys — four big biceps — come into the store. Midwestern look: muscled arms and protruding bellies, like pregnant women who are really into gym culture. I look over at Sandy to see if she's going to follow through. She's usually Front Zone/Greeter. But she's busy doling out shirts with her short arms and gives me this kind of pleading look.

"Hey guys, welcome to Redacted." I always fuck up greetings and it comes out like I'm at a family reunion for the estranged. "Anything I can help you find?"

The one wearing a black avenged sevenfold shirt shakes his head. "Nah man. We're just looking."

I nod. And then tell them like I just landed some juicy insider trading tips: "T-shirts are buy one, get one half-off."

"Cool, what's your name?"

"It's Vic."

"I'll let you know." He and his friend wander back left, past Sandy and towards the snapback hats.

I grab some of Sandy's folded shirts and take a peek out into the mall.

Redacted's walls are gray, and the floor-to-ceiling windows are so colonized by displays — mannequins garbed for a painfully cool summer — I have to poke my head out of the gate. I'm careful not to cross the Plate (a literal giant metal plate over the threshold) since we aren't allowed out without a manager's Pocket Check. When closing, I'll have mine checked by one of my Hosts. A few youngish women in leggings enter Forever 21 but the stragglers are packing it in. It's eight. Summerland Mall closes at nine and there's no reason we can't be out of here by nine-thirty.

I take the shirts back to the SHAM wall and rack them, then send Henshaw a quick text telling him I'll be there by 10. I get my phone back into my pocket just as Britt reemerges from the mythical backroom where we keep all sizes and colors except the one you want, and over next to the two guys standing by Hats. Said Hats being my AoR along with Shirts.

Britt puts her hands on her hips and calls me over. So I hustle to my Area of Responsibility. There's no reason for Britt to be here that would be good for me. She's got on Doc Martens but her hair is wrapped in a handkerchief so I know she isn't just checking in from being out and about. This is on purpose. Which means her boss, our district manager who works out of a desk in Kentucky, must have needed her. Britt is from California (thus the Wayfarers) unlike the rest of us. But she hates Indiana like the rest of us so theoretically we should get along better than we do.

"Vic." she says. "What's wrong with this picture?"

"I don't know."

She does this weird gesture with both arms that means *the whole hat wall*.

Then when I don't say anything she says, "The whole hat wall."

"I just reworked it today."

"Is this something else you don't know?"

Britt holds the Hats Planogram in front of my face and I promise it looks the same to me. I'm not sure what this says about my abilities as an essential member of the Redacted team.

"Yes?" I say.

She sighs and rubs her temples with the pads of her fingers. "What's your title?"

"Assistant Manager."

"Which means you're supposed to run this store the way I would if I were here."

All I want is to close and get out.

"You're not stupid, right? You went to college. Take a real look at this and tell me what's wrong."

A big guy and his slightly smaller (but still big) wife are taking drags on e-cigs, the kind with huge batteries, and before I can greet them Britt yells over and says *hi* and *please don't smoke those things in here*. The couple don't seem happy to put away the vapes. I use the few moments she's distracted to re-examine the wall. "Maybe the racks need to be straightened?"

She sighs. "I'm going on vacation and I'm scared, honestly. You're giving me night fright, Vic. What's my store going to look like when I get back? I can't have four hundred bucks walk out every week while the merchandising falls out of Best Practices. This store doesn't need both Merchandising Design and Loss Prevention filing reports, not when we're this close to top of District Nine."

"I'll fix it tomorrow."

She cocks her head and smiles. "You can fix it and still close on time. It doesn't take that long to close." She's finally sounded to herself the way she wants to. "This isn't what I came to talk to you about."

We move towards the Danger Door. I've already gotten two write-ups: one for being off the sales floor while vomiting in the Redacted toilet from Taco John's-inspired food poisoning, the second for leaving unfolded shirts in festive, mountainous stacks the day before Christmas Eve. Three warnings and you're gone. Then my dad gets his secret wish to not pay for me to become an educated person far from here.

The back room is a narrow corridor with a bathroom. It's packed floor to ceiling on both sides with racks and racks of glassware, sex toys, party lighting, shirts, more sex toys, pool toys, screwdrivers, angle brackets, and other seemingly random knickknacks. It's the basement of an amnesiac uncle who has loved every fad.

"So. Three grand, Vic. Just lost, with no apparent reason. Is this an accounting error, or should I be worried?"

"We can't be back here too long," I say.

"They can watch the store fine." Britt says, waving me off. "Darren is coming down for a check-in in two months. Right now that's the last week of Swim/Patriotic and right before we set Back to School. I'll be back from vacation, which means you'll have to do July 4th on your own. It can't be like that Hats wall shit. I need to know it will be right."

Whatever noise I make amounts to yes, I acknowledge your requirements for this, I admit your expertise in this, I reiterate my commitment to our shared enterprise.

"They're thinking of a Spectre Halloween pop-up this year with me in charge. That could be huge for me. I need you on board. I realize you're moving to New Jersey."

"Manhattan. It's Manhattan."

"Whatever." She waves towards Detroit. "East. The point is, just because you're moving, that doesn't mean I expect anything less than absolute commitment to best practices."

"Yes." When this doesn't relax her face, "Of course." I'm insulted she feels the need to press this onto me, like I'm not trying for a life of more money and to gain at least the rudiments of dignity.

"Other thing is: shrink. I don't want to come back from vacation and find out somebody walked out with a beer pong table and a cock ring. More important, money can't just disappear. This is a problem, Vic. An ongoing problem. You haven't caught a shoplifter the whole time you've been here. Money is going missing under your shift. We're approaching an LP violation. What am I supposed to think?"

*Shrink* means unaccounted-for merchandise and/or cash. Caused by either errors at the register or shoplifting.

"Could it be someone in the store?" I immediately regret asking this.

Britt gives me her most glacial stare. Cold and slow. "Always a possibility. That's pretty much it. Don't fuck up. And stop getting into fights on your days off. You look like a thug." Britt checks her watch.

The problem with Britt is that she's right. I don't belong here. I'm not qualified to run this store. Not because I don't know how, but because I haven't the slightest interest in doing so. Retail is real work for untold millions of people, but real work is what I'm avoiding by returning to academia. The idea of working some inglorious, meaningless job for the rest of my life fills my mouth with bile, even in this industry I understand and once thrived in. So while Britt is an honest person doing real work for not nearly as much pay as she deserves, I simply cannot bring myself to give a shit about this job.

I grab a ladder and drop it by the hats. Britt plays with the Office application on Register Two, checking time sheets. Then her email, then the new Bodily Fluid and Tissue Cleanup Compliance doc, some other distraction to keep me in sight while I get to work. I slide the Hat racks back and forth from the top to the bottom, stopping every third one to pull the rack and lay it on top of the ladder. Then I climb back to the hardware pile on the ground and pull two brackets and a shelf and go back up the ladder, where I slide brackets and shelf into slat wall before setting the rack of hats back on.

I've demonstrated my artistry.

Britt is waiting at the Plate. We do a Pocket Check on everyone, even if they're off the clock. It's a little like the TSA. She turns out her pockets, front and back, which I always find a little unnerving since I'm staring at asses. Britt pulls the jeans out of her boots, shows me the mesh bag she uses as a purse for work. She puts her sunglasses back on even though the sun has probably set and says, "See you later," before swishing out of the store back into the warm May air, carefree and oblivious as ever to the malevolent, Bath & Body Works scented cloud of psychic terror she brings wherever she goes.

One Spongebob and two Iron Man shirts are having some sort of three-way at the SHAM wall. The fat couple takes women's tops off the Stacey rack in the End Zone and unfold them, before stuffing them back unfolded.

One must imagine Sisyphus with a name tag.

# CHAPTER 9

By the time I finish the hat wall it's nine-twenty. I pop the drawer on Register 1 and quickly count out $400, and pull the other money into a deposit bag, then call Sandy over from finishing the shirts to double count while I count down Register Two. The way this works is, we keep $800 in the safe to start the day, $400 for each drawer and seal the rest in a plastic bag, which the next day's opener takes to the bank. If it's a particularly busy day we'll make extra deposit bags when we hit about $1,000 per drawer and lock those up too, just in case we get robbed. I'm supposed to watch her count, but I always turn my back and count the other drawer as a time savings. Britt says I'm not to close late, since I have the highest hourly rate in the store and if I do close late I'm costing the store money.

Sandy confirms my totals and we switch off. Both drawers are right so I enter the takings into the Paragon Office program. It comes back with an error: we're missing $500.

Panic hits me with a sharp jab to the ribs and I take the money out of the deposit bag and recount it. I double-check my totals, and they're correct. I have Sandy check it while I watch her closely.

"I got the same."

That brings our total cash theft up to $3,500. Well above any arbitrary threshold set by Home Office needed to justify further investigation. I can feel the eyes on me as we stand here, hear Britt's incredulous voice answering my protestations. No job means no check from my father. Without the check, I can't afford to relocate.

I stuff the money in the bags and walk through the Danger Door marked with its black and white HAZMAT symbol. There's nothing actually hazardous back here, the symbol is just "cool."

Sandy wedges the door open with her foot. "Hey. What's going on?"

"We're short." My hands shake as I punch the combination into the tiny safe and decide to lie. "Not a lot. But enough." I drop bags and jewelry keys into the safe, push in some excess shopping bags full of jewelry back in, and slam it shut.

"Oh shit. That's not good. What happens now?" Sandy follows me up to the registers to clock out. "Do you think it's just an error or something else?"

I pull out the Fiesta Folio (schedule/day planner) and check who worked. Patrick, the supervisor under me, opened, and Kyle came in for a bit too.

"Are you asking me if someone in the store is stealing?" I hit the lights.

"Wouldn't be the first time. Happened a lot at my old store."

We will wash this from my consciousness with alcohol in a couple of hours. For now I will grin as I surge with anxiety. I give her the same bloody rictus I put on for the customers.

"You know I can't answer that."

We lock the gate. The key is a mystical artifact to us. Only managers and the most entrusted Hosts receive keys, and they come with a commensurate bump in pay. We check each other's pockets, then say goodnight in the warm air of the parking lot.

I start my Lexus and turn on the stereo (gift, don't want to talk about it). I light a Camel Menthol after crushing the filter to make it extra minty then take a huge luxurious drag.

The smoke swirls around and out my open window into the sky and I lean back into the seat, and, for just a moment, feel the satisfaction of being employed and alive and tired and young on a summer night.

# CHAPTER 10

They used to keep a rotating installation in the lobby of the art and music building at Abboton University, usually just students, with one big piece from a local artist or maybe some big group project, all of it poorly lit behind glass display cases since if the art was left in the open the frat guys would desecrate it. When I'd pass by, which was often, I wouldn't give it a second glance, just because everything was painfully generic and besides, I didn't know shit about art anyways. Still don't.

But one time I saw this thing in the case as I came back downstairs. It was this like fucked up sculpture that looked vaguely like a person, a horrifying vision, the ugliest thing I'd ever seen, so of course I needed to step closer and take a look. There was no title, and only one name: "Kyle."

We had a class together that semester, up the stairs. History of the Methodist Church, meaningless filler trash they stuck in the hottest little room in the art building. He was, for the most part, a very quiet and studious boy with floppy hair. But that day, the day I saw that sculpture in the lobby, he was a little different.

If you had an event to promote at AU you could write down the name, date, time, and location in a corner of the whiteboard and box it off with the word "keep" and for about a week you'd be good. No one would bother it. It was mostly frats who used this method of advertising, boasting about their keggers where freshmen would get alcohol poisoning and the women would be groped, prodded, fondled.

So that day, when I came into the classroom and took my seat in the back, Kyle was drawing a particularly ornate ad in the corner of the whiteboard, complete with flowers and skulls, that just said *DRAG SHOW: KEEP*, with the date and location scrawled all tiny in the very bottom. And when he got done, he capped the marker, stood on the teacher's desk, and stamped his combat boots twice.

"Attention," he said. "I will be performing this Friday at Someplace Else. It is an unconventional drag performance. If you haven't attended a drag performance in a while because all the trash queens in this mole on God's ass can't even lip sync to 'I Will Survive' without tripping in their stripper heels, I assure you this will not be utter garbage."

I had never heard him speak before. He was wearing a lot of eyeliner and leggings and the most tattered sweater I'd ever seen, and he spoke in a high, lilting voice. I'd never seen anyone quite like him before. The gays I was used to were either hopeless closet cases or scruffy dudes in Wranglers who believed they were blessed with aesthetic taste by virtue of being born homosexual. Kyle was different, still is different. You don't get to that point by 18 in a town like this. The boy had talent and presence and the reckless abandon to go with it.

Two fratty guys chuckled by the door. Kyle ignored them. "I realize that most of you don't give a shit. However, self-promotion is nine-tenths of any artistic endeavor."

The teacher walked through the door, tubby little guy, and stopped short. Wasn't sure how to proceed.

"Thank you for your time," Kyle said. "I look forward to none of you attending, you pack of philistines."

He hopped off and landed on an abandoned pencil with a

crunch before swishing back to his seat, right next to mine. The teacher took his place behind the desk and looked at the ad in the corner of the board, picking up an eraser and shaking his head.

I piped up. "I don't think you want to erase your only gay student's advertisement, sir."

The prof turned on me, and looked at Kyle. He put the eraser down.

Kyle didn't thank me, of course. He doesn't thank anyone. I leaned over and whispered to him. "What time is it? The show, I mean. You didn't say."

Kyle looked me down, ever so subtly. He thinks he's real slick about it, but I can see him judging me whenever he looks at me. I dress trashy, not sexy trashy either. Casual trashy. "It's at 7, but God knows when I'll go on."

"Cool, thanks," I said. I turned back to the textbook and didn't say anything for the rest of the session.

He didn't expect me to show up, but I did. Don't get me wrong, I avoided Someplace Else. Sure, everyone there was more or less discreet, but it was far easier to blend in with the beer-crushing bros and preppy club kids I've always been forced next to.

They have a decent sized stage and dancefloor, and they do drag shows every week. It's always the same handful of queens and their same collection of fans and hags, all of them so utterly boring. It's not a young crowd, and it's not a cool one. It's just the accumulated gay men and women who have nowhere else to go.

They went through the usual lineup, what I assume was the usual anyway. It was all boring. Madonna, Cher. Someone did Lady Gaga as if that shit wasn't already spent. All of them with names like Ivana Spankoff or whatever. I spent a lot of it outside smoking, unbothered by men who read me, accurately, as straight and unattractive.

"And now, for the first time ever, give it up for SPECIAL K."

She gets on stage, and her costume is like none other. It's wildly androgynous, this bizarre futuristic fetish getup, all straps and angular pieces of rubber and pleather. This was before *RuPaul's Drag Race* started spreading all these extreme looks to box wine drinking normies. Drag queens at this time and place were all pretty subdued, just a little over the top, almost as if they were trying to pass. As if going too far would cause some invisible monster to smack your hands away from the eyeshadow palette, tell you to stop before you disrupted the mores of the third-largest and most conservative city in Indiana.

And the actual show, my god. She chose an electronic track with female vocals and a dark sound that called to mind dingy clubs, converted warehouses, the aroma of dry sweat from manual labor. It was the most unsettling and beautiful noise I'd ever heard. The lyrics spoke of loss, and an indecent erotic longing, at once a banger and the kind of thing I'd cry to alone in my room with a bottle.

Kyle danced like she was some kind of machine, a terrifying post-industrial vision, drawing inexplicably from Martha Graham of all things. She danced in a way that recalled a dank German club, summoning us erotically, unmistakably feminine, inviting a room of gay men towards something they didn't want. She wasn't playing a woman, but she became one. One that didn't exist in Abboton, but did and would elsewhere. The whole thing was three minutes, but felt like it lasted forever. I wanted it to last forever. I was entranced, smitten. This was unlike anything I'd ever seen. From this vantage point it was probably pretty conventional, just an average fusion of performance art and drag aesthetics, but in that time it was glorious.

The crowd didn't really care for it, of course. There was very little applause, and the hostess made a snide comment when she ducked out the stage door. I hung around for a while afterwards but didn't see Kyle anywhere, so I texted some classmates and figured out there was a party at some theatre house a couple blocks from campus.

When I got to the party the hostess was handing out flowers and demanding we all put them in our hair. I had grown mine out just enough to wear it would stay, and I took two, feeling invigorated by the energy I'd gleaned from Kyle's performance. The music was all trip-hop and new wave occasionally punctuated by show tunes for the actors to belt out in unison. It wasn't really my scene but I was in a bit of a daze, unable to really process what I'd seen. Kyle had gotten to me, and I hated him for it.

And then, I saw him. He was out of costume, wearing a ragged t-shirt and smoking on the balcony with some butch girl with an equally tattered haircut. I wasn't sure what to say, or even if I should approach. But then I figured fuck it, and walked up to him, pulling a square out of my own pack.

"Got a light?" I asked.

He pulled his out with effortless grace and lit mine without looking at me. "Only pretty girls get their cigarettes lit."

"What a line," his companion said. She stuck out a limp hand to me. "Amory."

"Thanks for coming," Kyle said, still not looking at me.

"It was amazing," I said. "It blew my fucking mind, dude."

Amory laughed and punched his arm. "Told you! It's just these rubes that don't know anything. I like this guy."

They were both clearly drunk, and of course so was I. There's nothing to do around here but fuck and farm, so everyone drinks heavily and it's weird if you don't. I've never met a sober person in Abboton.

Kyle laughed, painfully. "Have you considered that he's a rube as well? He sits next to me in class, and says nothing."

"Neither do you," I pointed out.

"What is your major, V?" he asked me.

"Comp Lit. And I've got a 4.0." I was drunk and boasting,

eager to make an impression on him. "I only dress like this because I don't give a shit."

"I like how you dress," he said. "I don't think you're a rube."

Amory let out some kind of low sound. "Excuse me. I need to freshen my nose." She slipped away back into the house.

Kyle exhaled. "I have a joint if you want to smoke."

We went around the side of the house, under the trees in the dark where no one could see us. Kyle was wearing wedge sneakers and there were wet fall leaves on the lawn. He put a hand on my arm to steady himself, and I felt a despised thrill go through me. The joint was lit, real dirt weed. But we were poor college kids, so what can you do?

"I meant what I said before. About you being amazing," I said. "I mean, the show being amazing."

"I'm sure you did."

"You're a hell of an artist. I really dug your sculpture. The one in the art building."

"Do you make art, V?"

"I don't. I have no creative ability whatsoever. I'm just a huge nerd."

We were killing time, really. We both knew what came next, under the influence, and as alone as one can be at a party. He kissed me first, sloppy and wet. I kissed him back. It wasn't my first time, not by a long shot, but it had been a while. We'd been at it for a couple minutes, groping each other, kissing deeper and deeper, before I finally pushed him away.

"I'm not gay," I said. "I have a girlfriend." Which was mostly true.

"I don't give a shit," he said, and he kissed me again.

And honestly, I didn't either.

# CHAPTER 11

"We're seriously not going anywhere?" I ask Henshaw as he turns his old Buick onto Weinbach. "I mean are we really not going someplace. Really going out."

"We're going to Lex's. You're just looking to get laid."

Henshaw, the big meat wall, always thinks he's such a playboy, such a slick guy. And I'm just sitting here thinking to myself, *Erica told me your dick curves to the left.*

"If I was just looking to get laid," I say, "I have my ways."

Henshaw shifts his girth and adjusts his underwear. "Uh huh. Hand me my cigarettes, would you? Glove compartment."

I pull the pack out from where they sit next to Henshaw's pistol before rolling down the window and lighting one. I took two big, heavy pulls of booze out of my trunk before I banged on Henshaw's door so I'm already feeling good.

In the side mirror I can see my alma mater's quad and front entrance and the illuminated stone slab on the corner that says *Abboton University* in fine Romanesque letters, and it makes me a little sad to know I won't be going back, as well as desperate to return to the academy's dry, heaving bosom.

I get a text from Erica. *Coming over?* Because I said maybe, but didn't say I wouldn't.

*I can't hanging out with Henshaw. Maybe others.*

*Oh. I wish you'd told me*

For a moment I have the mix of guilt and a little horniness and I consider telling Henshaw to turn around. Instead I type *Well sorry* and silence my iPhone before putting it back in my pocket.

"Who's that?" he asks.

I say nothing, still fearful of his wrath, and pocket my phone.

Inside Liquor Locker we stare at the cases of beer.

"PBR?" I ask.

"We're not hipsters. Keystone?" Henshaw asks.

"I don't feel like vomiting."

"Busch?"

"And I'm not getting ready to fuck my sister."

"Heineken?"

"And I'm not getting ready to fuck *your* sister in a convertible."

"Come on," Henshaw groans. "Pick something already."

"High Life."

"Hell no, I'm not drinking that. You're such a hipster."

"Okay. How about actual liquor?"

We drift over to the half gallons and try to make a quality to value calculation. $11 for Kamchatka versus $13 for Dark Eyes. I try to summon memories of hangovers past. Tomorrow comes into clearer focus and that anxiety starts to crossfade with my anxiety about not going out and getting old. I try to make myself calm down but it doesn't work.

"We should go somewhere."

"Dude," Henshaw says. "I only have 15 bucks. That won't get me anything."

"We can get nickel beers at Moody's."

I pick up a half gallon of Dark Eyes and walk it back to the counter.

"I.D. Please," the clerk says.

I give him my license so he can thumb it and squint at my picture. "This you?" he asks.

I know it's me, and he knows it's me, and I wonder, as I often do when this happens, if it's because I look kind of Middle Eastern in my I.D. photo. "Yeah," I say.

"What's your license number?"

"I don't know."

"What's your birthday?"

"July 23, 1989"

"What's the expiration date?"

Henshaw comes up behind me. "What's going on?"

"I dunno." I say to the clerk, "It's like 2016? I got it after I turned 18."

The clerk looks at me and then up at the six-foot-seven-inch tower of Henshaw and hands me back my I.D.

# CHAPTER 12

Founded by Frederick Abbot in 1812, Abboton has a population of ~125,000, a metro area (commonly referred to as *Kentuckiana* or the *Tri-State*) population of ~300,00, is home to three NYSE companies: Magnum Plastic And Rubber, Greenwise Financial, Parker Pilgrim Pharmaceuticals, a riverboat casino, the worst public library system in the state, the second largest street fair in the United States, the South Side Germanic Social Society's Thunder Fest, and my dysfunctional and abusive multiethnic nuclear family unit.

# CHAPTER 13

Lex sits in the corner of his dirty sectional — dirty like his shirt with two killer clowns on it, dirty like how he smells. "What are you doing?"

"Making a road drink," I say, pouring a few shots of vodka plus the remainder of the sweet and sour into a single-use orange juice bottle.

"You're crazy, man." Lex peels a cup off the ever-crusty living room table and takes a drink. Everything smells like meat.

"You're the only person I know who would do that and not puke," he says.

"You took half a pint of Admiral Nelson in my car last week."

He laughs and I grin. We've each had a vodka sour, and I'm starting to feel drunk, like really drunk and I can tell I'm getting talkative and I tell myself *careful*...

I grab an empty pack of Parliaments. "Whose are these?" I ask.

"I dunno," Lex says. "Maybe Trina's, don't remember. She and Slow came by Tuesday. I don't remember anything that happened." He takes a moment and thinks. "We made a pitcher of Caribou Lous and I hit Slow's e-cig hard. I don't remember nothing."

"I hate e-cigs." I take a pull on my real cigarette to make a point. The best thing about Lex's house is smoking inside.

"I love them. He's got this tropical shit in it, tastes like Froot Loops."

Henshaw comes back from his third phone call of the night. "I swear, dude. Kyle couldn't wipe his taint without me." He adjusts his pants and looks at the bottle in my hand. "You're not bringing that in the car. I can't believe I'm doing this."

"I can't really either," Lex says. "I thought we were gonna stay here but I can't pass up nickel beer Friday." He gets up to grab what money he has left out of his room.

I turn the Parliament pack over in my hand again. "I don't believe anyone smoked these. No one smokes Parliaments." I'm getting animated in that early drunk sort of way. "No one."

"I know, right," Henshaw says. "People smoke Camels or Marlboros, and that's it. Maybe the hipsters have a few American Spirits with their PBR. They should come in a two pack."

Lex comes back in the living room now wearing an Insane Clown Posse hat and a *fucking* chain and I groan inside but I don't say anything. "Or Pall Malls if you're broke or cheap," I say.

"Or Newports if you're a nigger," Lex says and Henshaw laughs and I know he's joking but I can feel my blood pressure rise and the rage pulse through my head and take me away from myself because Lex is *white* and I'm *not-white* I'm *biracial* and after the booze and the clerk I feel it more than usual but I remind myself that Lex is *just kidding* and I shouldn't be offended and these are my friends.

# CHAPTER 14

It costs five bucks to get into Moody's on a Friday night and from there you can go to any of the three bars inside and get a half pint of Keystone Light for a nickel. Usually I just hand them a quarter. Henshaw didn't bring change so he breaks a five and it pisses him off. He didn't let me bring the road drink so I'm feeling a little aggravated and considering the aftershocks of the casual drop of *nigger with the hard "r"* I feel a little vindicated. The place is always full of college students and country people in work boots, two groups that don't mix and don't attempt to mix but instead congregate in oily pools at various corners and tables in the vast, dimly lit, and thumping space. I see this kid named Sayid over in the corner with some Saudi guys I knew in college. They're drinking Jägerbomb. I have a brief flashback to me and Lex sitting in the parking lot of this very bar eating Rally's and we got into it with this random country girl in a Ford Explorer because I said "Have a good night," and she thought I was trying to pick her up. I feel kind of jealous that Sayid and his buddies can afford actual drinks and brand-name alcohol, but then I remember that most of the international students at Abboton don't have jobs so that cheers me up a bit.

I move past the mechanical bull and look out on the dancefloor where about 12 people are getting down to "A$$" by Big Sean and I kind of want to dance but I haven't since I broke up with Beth who used to do roller derby and really liked dancing.

Lex swings by with two beers and posts up next to me. He drinks out of both while his head bobs along to the music. He stares at a white girl in leopard-print leggings on the floor and he turns and yells something at me but I can't understand so I just nod my head and, after an appropriate wait, laugh. I return to the right-side bar and get another beer and pull out my iPhone and compose a tweet about creepers and hit send. I have 90 followers which means I've lost two and I panic for a minute. I go back to find Lex at one of the tables across from the dance floor.

"Man I need to get laid," he says.

"Are you drinking out of both of those beers?" I ask.

"Oh god." I follow Lex's eyes to Henshaw, gesturing wildly at a brunette in a long skirt.

"He's doing his thing," I say. "Creating value."

Henshaw and I smoke cigarettes on the brightly lit patio overlooking the riverwalk while I ask how it went with the girl. He gives a non-committal noise before trying to chat with a guy in a Lynyrd Skynyrd tee (but not one we sell) complaining about the music. I can make out a little Arabic at the end of the patio as a few guys banter and throw their heads back, laughing and making a lot of noise. These townie kids smoking Pall Malls give them stink eye, especially this white boy in a camo hat who's particularly pissed off. They're all taking big pulls of Bud Light even though Keystone is the one that's a nickel on Fridays.

I want to watch but am not drunk enough so I flick my cigarette into the street and go back inside to splurge on a dime's worth of Keystone and a Jägerbomb. I notice Sayid at the bar and slide over. "You feeling it?"

"Good man, good." Sayid is tall and the good-looking kind

of bald and Syrian and I can never understand his accent but I always know what he's saying. "Got a job at Microsoft."

"Wow."

"Yeah. Big going away party! Big party this weekend."

I can't tell if he's inviting or just telling me so I nod and bump Jagerbombs with him.

Lex and Henshaw are in a booth arguing so I go to the restroom, dodging the usual moat of piss surrounding the urinals. Two frat guys in button-up shirts stumble out talking about this bartender in a bikini top.

"They're like A cups."

"I don't give a shit."

I piss and wash my hands, fighting the broken and empty soap dispenser. The whole place stinks of urine and Axe body spray. Everything tilts and I shift my weight back and forth and shake my head. I wish I had some coke.

Suddenly I'm back in the booth, clutching two more beers I don't remember ordering and drinking from both. I motion to Henshaw and we go outside to smoke, this time accompanied by Lex. The DJ plays "Save a Horse, Ride A Cowboy."

"I hate this new country, man." Lex says. "I love me some Johnny Cash, that's real country."

"You okay?" Henshaw asks me. Sayid is loudly conversing with his friends outside and smoking imported cigarettes. The rednecks yell at them to be quiet but the Saudi kids don't listen.

The taste of the beer gives me life that goes out of me and back to the city and I can feel it, pumping. You can see the Ohio River across the street from the patio, stretching to the unseen Kentucky side and all the woods and dark things oozing through the water. There's industrial-strength air conditioners at the casino hotel nearby that throb all night, adding to that feeling of latent mechanical life while the casino itself, a converted riverboat, sits quietly on the water, floating stagnant in gaudy lighting. The music changes back to Kanye West. "Niggas in Paris." The beat mixes with the buzzing of the casino and I can feel the pulse, from the cigarette to me out to the casino and back into the music and into everyone else.

Sayid mounts the table and starts dancing, and the guy in the camo hat reaches up and grabs him and yells at him to get down and Sayid, he falls and the camo guy punches him and the others get involved and now there's this wave of humanity flowing towards us tables and chairs are going everywhere and I hear Lex yell *"Oh shit,"* and there's blood on the concrete, red where a second ago nothing, and there's pounding and beating and slapping and yelling and I can hear Kanye slurring and the cops are already running over from the swank casino hotel and we're out of the bar and on the street and I laugh in the backseat of the Buick with the windows down as the orange sodium lights fly by on the expressway and the radio blares as we do 70 in a 50 at one in the morning.

# CHAPTER 15

Henshaw shuffles through the bag of Taco Bell on his coffee table and removes a wet square wrapped in yellow paper. The table is glass, and there are three orange pill bottles on it that I can't read but don't want to pick up, since that would be rude and I'm far gone but not that much. I think about asking him for a pill but decide against it. He squirts three packets of hot sauce onto the taco and takes a huge bite. I take a drink out of the juice bottle I squirreled away in the backseat of his car.

"I thought I told you not to bring that in my car," he says.

"You know I have a chronic disregard for authority."

"You're gonna throw up."

"Nah," I say, sipping. I've almost forgotten about the theft.

Lex plays these 90s rock tracks I kind of remember but don't really. 90s music is one of the main things he and I have in common. I don't remember why we came to Henshaw's house instead of Lex's, but I'm also pretty sure I wasn't asked.

Henshaw's place is only a ten-minute car ride from Lex's, through some back roads in a more sparsely populated neighborhood. It was a nicer place once upon a time, but several foreclosures and the death of some elderly homeowners has put it on the same downward slide most streets around here are experiencing. This is the only place Henshaw could afford to buy a house. Every inch of it is his, financed at a competitive rate by Old National Bank. He has set down roots just as I am tearing mine up. He has beaten the curve, thrown off the landlord's yoke. And by renting to Kyle, he's technically become a landlord himself. Already he's done something I likely never will.

Real shame that he decorated it like he owns it, though. The top of Henshaw's bookshelf is lined with Jagermeister bottles. There's an old Korn poster on the wall and it reminds of Tripp pants and I laugh because those are always funny.

"Play 'Thrash Unreal,'" I say.

"Why?" Lex asks.

"'Cause I heard it at work today."

"This is my Spotify."

"Play it, fucker."

"Fuck you." But he laughs and puts the song on.

Henshaw fishes out a bean burrito. I start singing along, happy at first then kind of watery. I wish I could light a cigarette but this isn't Lex's place.

A bedroom door opens and closes and Kyle walks in, skinny, dyed faux hawk, tank top and pajama pants. I've never seen him this casual and I seize up immediately as I remember first how drunk I am and then the missing 500-something bucks. He nods to us and goes through the curtain into the kitchen, then comes back with a glass of water.

"Didn't mean to wake you," Henshaw says. He gives me a look.

"Wasn't asleep," Kyle mumbles. He walks over to one of the pill bottles, shakes a couple into his palm, and plops onto the couch next to me. "Why are you playing this song?"

"Victor wanted to hear it."

Kyle groans and looks at me. "I'm so sick of hearing it. I wish I was far away.." He slumps further into the chair. "I have to work tomorrow. This sucks."

"Me too. Do you want a ride?"

"I hate Taco Bell." He sniffs. "Why is it always tacos with you people?"

Henshaw's phone rings and he goes outside to stand on the porch. Kyle leans over to me and whispers. He smells like sandalwood and pillows. I remember it well.

"If you want me to introduce you to my friend who is totally hot for you," he says, "then you need to go tell Shaw that you're fucking Erica. Also, you need to stop fucking Erica."

"She's been texting me all night, and I didn't go find her," I say. "Isn't that enough?"

"No, it isn't. Go tell him."

For a moment I wonder if this is Kyle's way of figuring out if I'm still interested in him. He does like to play games. But my thoughts are thick and slow. Instead of thinking I follow Henshaw and sit on the steps, steadying my torso through sheer will. Nights like this one, I swear I can hear something over the drunken ringing in my ears, a low hum or a dull mechanical beating heart from far off keeping time. I can feel something like a confession pressing against my tongue to the back of my teeth, but I can't find the words and just give up.

"Alright. I'll drop it off tomorrow." He locks his phone. "I knew there was a reason I didn't like Moody's," Henshaw says. "All the bar fights."

"There's one every time I've been there," I say. "A lot of them about race."

"How was that racially motivated? They were just drunk and mad at the guy dancing on the table."

"Dancing on a table isn't a reason. He's Arab."

"Not everything is about race."

"This was." I reach up and rub my shaved head. "I don't want to have this talk."

"You okay?"

"Someone stole from the drawer. Which means, worst case, that I'm out on my ass." I stare at my phone's screen, blurry with smeared taco sauce. "Why did you bring me here? I shouldn't be drunk around my Hosts."

"Hosts? It's a fuck off retail job. Who cares? You should quit. Come work with me."

"My father won't help me out if I quit. No grad school."

"Ah. Yeah. Can't anger daddy or else we won't be able to move to the big city. Then you'd have to get a real job like the rest of us little people. How much cash do you have, anyway? Will you make it in the big city, or will you have to whore your pretty little ass out?"

"I'm broke. Does Kyle owe you money?"

"A little for rent. You think he robbed you?"

"Maybe."

# CHAPTER 16

In the middle of the night or more like almost dawn I jerk awake and stare into the darkness. Something looks back at me, a hole in the universe, the *thing* that haunts me at hours like this when my brain can almost but not quite touch on something. He's come to tell me what he always does, silently, efficiently: *Something has gone wrong.*

*My father lays his rifle across the bed and tells my mother "One of us is going to die tonight."*

# CHAPTER 17

Erica. She's texting me again as I pull into the mall parking lot, Kyle riding shotgun.

*I need a couple hundred bucks. You can swing that, right? I'll pay you back.*

*No, I really can't. I'm not an ATM. I already told Henshaw that we've been fucking, so you got nothing over me.*

*This doesn't have anything to do with that. I'm in a really bad spot, my roommate is pissed, and I really need the money right now, today. After our little talk I wouldn't come to you if I didn't absolutely have to this is humiliating enough as it is so please please just help me out okay. Or if you'd rather I can tell my boyfriend about how you paid for my abortion and we weren't even sure whose it was. Would you rather I do that? Cause if I can't pay my bills then what the fuck is the point?*

*Okay wow.*

*Please don't make me beg. I already asked Henshaw and he said no.*

"Shit."

Kyle looks away from his phone at me over his giant knock-off Ray-Bans and pulls one be-sneakered shoe onto the seat. "What's wrong?"

"Get your feet off the leather."

"It's pleather."

*This is literally the last time. I promise, baby. Just give me enough to get by.*

I look up my father's number in then clear it out at least a half-dozen times, each time remembering that voice, the vocal frown, getting turned down for help over and over, each time carrying a deeper sense of disapproval and that same message that something is wrong with me that wasn't wrong with him, or his father, or his father's father, and that until it is rectified I am not his son, just a grudging obligation.

"If you don't need me," Kyle says. "I gotta get to work."

I finally text him, asking for the money. I say it's for a blown-out tire. He responds with something closer to a letter than an SMS. *I would expect that you'd understand I'm offering you a lot as it is. Given the nature of my contribution to your graduate career, I think it's only fair that you pay for your car, especially since you will be leaving it with me. Life will offer many challenges, and incidentals like this...*

And that's all I need to read. I know the rest by heart.

# CHAPTER 18

"This really is the last time, I swear," Erica says. At least she had the decency to come meet me at the parking lot.

I hand her the money. It's a cash advance up to the limit on my very last credit card, just under a couple hundred bucks plus fees. "We're through."

"Don't leave it like that," she pouts. Her hands count the money, too quickly. "This is like, $180."

My phone rings again. "Hang on a second."

I put it on speakerphone.

"Hello Mr. Adewale. I'm calling from Solutions International in regards to your account. Your total debt is now in the amount of $12,582 and if we cannot receive payment we will be forced to take other measures."

I hang up the phone. We stare at each other in silence.

"Is that why you stole the money?" Erica asks me. Her voice is small.

"I've got to get to work," I say. "I didn't steal the money. And if I did, I certainly wouldn't be talking to you about it."

# CHAPTER 19

Some part of me wants to go to Redacted early, the part of me that feels bosses should be involved in their employees all the time. But I'm not a boss, more a messenger, an intermediary, and with an hour to kill I could do more for my own mental health by not going in there.

So instead I sit down at an empty table in the food court and pull out my phone. The cops that beat up a black guy in Indianapolis, they haven't been arrested, and people are angry about that. There's nothing new on *Vice* or *Salon* and there's a sense of dread at the fact that the Internet is moving slow, a dread compounded by my lack of funds while surrounded by stores and restaurants. I open my photos and scroll to one of the ones Erica sent me the other night.

A tray slams down on the table in front of me and I jump, reflexively ready to fight. Kyle sits down across from me.

"Hi," he says, sea green crop top hanging off his shoulder, hair in badly dyed orange quiff. "Why are you still here? You don't come in until 2, you should take a nap."

I put my phone on the table face down. "I have nothing better to do. How's Britt?"

He rolls his lined eyes and spears some orange chicken

with his fork. "She's all freaking out because we got shipment in. I can't with her some days. Patrick will tell you all about it, he's getting the worst of it right now. I'm supposed to dye her hair tonight but I'm not looking forward to it anymore."

"You look a lot better than you did this morning."

He chews, swallows. "So do you."

"I look like shit."

"Well, I figured we were telling each other lies, as usual."

A woman about my age in all black with a ratty black haircut to match sits down next to me with a tray of chicken nuggets and waffle fries. "They don't give us a discount anymore," she says. I can smell the pot smoke in her hair and hear the cigarettes in her voice. "I'm going to have to find a less homophobic place to get chicken." She glances towards me. "Hey, Vic."

"How do you know my name again?"

She stops in the middle of opening a tiny plastic tub of honey mustard and her bored eyes almost light up. "You don't remember me, do you?"

It's always weird and slightly aggravating when strangers call you by the name on your tag, like they know you or something, like they've earned the right to use your name when you haven't even introduced yourself.

But then I remember. I'm not wearing my tag. "You look familiar," I say.

"I shouldn't be surprised." She finishes opening the packet and dunks a chunk of all-natural white meat in it. "You were pretty drunk."

I feel the familiar thrill and slight embarrassment when someone I don't know recognizes me. "Should I remember you?"

"How do you know Kyle?"

"We went to AU, he was a couple years below me. For a while anyway. What about it?"

Kyle reaches over and takes one of her waffle fries. "Oh please, don't do this to him."

"Stop eating my food. Don't tell him my name. I want to see if he remembers. No, don't take another one, you should have gotten fries if you wanted them instead of that shitty mall lo mein."

I find it hard to believe I wouldn't remember someone like this, since I keep a mental record of all my rivals and enemies along with their sins and vices and how vile they were and if I should ever talk to them again.

"Sorry. I really don't know."

"Come on, Amory," Kyle says. "He means well."

She throws her balled-up paper straw sleeve at him. Kyle makes a kind of half-apologetic shrug, but he's obviously amused.

And then I remember. The night of his performance. Smoking on the balcony. We had flowers in our hair.

"We went to college together."

"I'm not talking to you," she says. She gives me a sniff. "At least you don't smell like tequila this time. God, you were so drunk."

"You work here?"

"PacSun. It sucks. We just lost a manager because he was shoplifting. Prick."

"Yeah," Kyle says. He steals another fry and she slaps his hand. "We've been having," he stops and looks at me and covers his mouth with the slapped hand. "Oh shit."

"Shrink's been up," I tell Amory. "Not a good sign."

Kyle's look has become guarded and his muscles tense, mostly because I shouldn't have told her that, especially when a sales associate like him is present. "Yeah. It's going around."

Amory shrugs. "It's not just y'all. Zumiez, Hot Topic, all the little emo fucker stores are getting hit."

"You don't think it's internal?" I ask.

"Do you?"

"No comment." I pick up my phone and unlock it, the photo of Erica's tits in full view on my screen.

Amory glances over. "She's got a nice rack."

Kyle buses his half-eaten tray. "I gotta get back. Smoke?"

We go outside the front doors and stare into the endlessly crowded and baking expanse of the parking lot

"I'm trying to quit," Amory says.

"Good." I light mine. "It's bad for you. Besides, more for the rest of us."

She pulls the cigarette out of my mouth and puts it in hers, drawing slowly then letting it out. She hands it back to me. "I knew you weren't gay. You always stare at my tits."

She turns and waves to Kyle before heading back inside.

"You kind of were staring at her tits." Kyle says.

"I should know better shouldn't I?" I slide down the concrete wall to squat on my ankles.

"V, so long as you don't stare at my ass while we're working, we'll all get along fine."

It would be nice to remember her now. I wish I did.

# CHAPTER 20

The phone rings and I pick up. "Thank you for calling Redacted, where every day is a party. This is Vic, how can I help you?"

"Hey Vic," says the voice on the line. "It's Darren. Is Britt there?"

Darren. Our District Manager. Britt's boss. "No, she's on lunch."

"Have her call me. Bye."

Britt swoops back into the store with a bag of Chick-Fil-A, back to work, taking off her sunglasses.

"Darren just called," I say.

"Good."

# CHAPTER 21

Saturdays at the store present a different kind of challenge, not because there's more work but just because the volume we do is insane. The sheer press of human flesh and odors packing itself into a store on the weekend causes enthusiasm and angst among even the most seasoned retail worker. Sales goals double or triple. Contests are won and lost. Killing it on the weekends can save a store that does crap during the week.

Stores like ours.

This particular Saturday isn't any worse even though the nice weather makes it feel worse and brought in even more business.

"Look mommy!" says some kid in a Disney Princess shirt, pointing at the disco lights.

"Yes dear," says her obviously exhausted mother. She, her husband, her friend, her son, and her daughter clutch ice creams in various states of decay. As they enter from the mall I spit the script at them over the din of the mall and the banging Deadmau5 music:

"Hey guys, how are you doing? Anything I can help you find? Okay, well let me know, shirts are buy one, get one half off."

My job most any Saturday is to stay in the front, help customers, restock what gets brought up front, and above all watch for shoplifters.

"Hey guys, how are you doing? Anything I can help you find? Okay, well let me know, shirts are buy one, get one half off."

The store has three zones: back, middle, front. One manager in each. Today, like most Saturdays, it's Britt in the back, Patrick in the middle since he opened (openers come in alone and have to watch the whole store for a couple hours until the mid-shift manager, in this case Britt, comes in), and me up front. At this point I'm alone up here since it's still early, but I close with Kyle later when he comes back for the second half of the split shift he had to take since we lost someone last week. Mostly I need to keep an eye on a display of light-up speakers near the front. There's eight in the stack. They've been one of our most popular items, even since a video of them went viral and spread through various social media networks. As such, they remain one of our most shoplifted items.

Only managers can catch shoplifters. The company has given us a handy acronym for how to catch thieves:

**Approach**: The suspect must approach the merchandise.

**Conceal**: The suspect must conceal the merchandise.

**Exit**: The suspect crosses the lease line (front door) while in possession of the merchandise.

**Stop**: The manager must stop the suspect and take them in the back for processing.

**ACES! Stop The Crime Every Time!**

"Hey guys, how are you doing? Anything I can help you find? Okay, well let me know, shirts are buy one, get one half off."

Signs of potential shoplifters include but are not limited to: hoodies, baseball caps, strollers, out-of-season clothes (winter coats in summer), traveling in packs, repeat customers, poor hygiene, and looking around a lot. Much like banks and the police department, Redacted does not allow racial profiling, and anyone caught doing so can be written up for creating a hostile workplace.

I've never caught a shoplifter.

"Just go with your gut," Britt told me in training. She isn't happy with my lack of performance. It doesn't look good that I've been here so long and still haven't caught anybody. Besides prosecuting thieves and banning them from the store, corporate can and will sue them for up to fifty times the price of the stolen merchandise. Loss Prevention (LP) is one of the biggest parts of our job. Catching one shoplifter deters another, and considering the nature of our product we attract a lot of shoplifters.

"Hey guys, how are you doing? Anything I can help you find? Okay, well let me know, shirts are buy one, get one half off."

Britt's standing in the back of the store eyeing a few teenagers in neon leggings and dog collars. I watch a couple teenage dudes mess with shot glasses as I micro-straighten the front wall of Music shirts. One of them palms a glass that says "SLUT". He puts his hand to his side and looks around and sees me staring him down. He puts the glass down and I inwardly curse myself for not being more discreet.

"I mean, deterring them is great," Britt said to me on my first day. "But you've got to catch somebody. I've already caught four people this year." Her techniques mostly involve standing near people who look poor or ethnic and just watching them. "It's not a race thing," she said. "I'll watch anyone who looks suspicious. I'm not racist, I'm from California. Diversity is a big thing for me. I mean you're what, Puerto Rican?"

"No," I said. "I'm black."

Today she's wearing new jeans and one of our Stacey shirts and her trademark pinup hairstyle. My friends think she's crazy hot but I can't see it. I don't fuck people I work with, and I make a big deal about not fucking people I work with as though it's a virtue and not common sense. Her boyfriend is hot in a dirty, rough trade way so I suppose she must have some appeal.

A scene kid wants a pair of plugs, so I grab them out of the case and upsell him a second pair for half off. I check him out as more people flow in and out from the mall. The family with the ice cream slowly picks their way through the store, accumulating more and more stuff. The daughter's chocolate cone is slowly losing structural integrity.

After I ring the kid out and get his email for a 25% off coupon, I turn around to find Britt right behind me. "Hi!" she says, smiling.

"Hey," I say.

"Back to the front of the store. And make sure you greet everyone." She turns to a teenager checking out the industrial bars in the jewelry case. "Have you seen this one? It's got a little American flag on it. Perfect for July 4th. It's the only one we've gotten in."

We are required to greet (and pitch an offer) and re-approach (and pitch a different offer) to every customer under pain of a poor grade from our secret shoppers. Poor secret shops mean no raises and a critical eye cast upon management.

Patrick's talking to one of his old high school friends, and I can't help but notice that I haven't seen him re-approach anyone. He's a weak link and everyone knows it, but he's just so sweet and cute and self-loathingly gay everyone kind of treats him too well. His recent promotion to Sales Supervisor caused a bit of a stir since older, more experienced Hosts were passed over, two of whom quit in protest. My opinion wasn't solicited in the hiring process.

I approach a customer in his zone and pitch some jewelry to break up his convo. "Look, you need to move around a bit, okay? See if you can straighten the middle shirts, too."

"I know," he says. "I was just talking to my pals. From the fire show."

I grab his beanie off his head, almost snagging the industrial bar in his ear. "Just make sure you're keeping an eye out." I toss the hat back to him and he smiles and dives back into the crowd, weaving through and chatting up potential sales. I look up and see Britt in the back, hands on hips. She waves me back to the front of the store.

"Hey guys, how are you doing? Anything I can help you find? Okay, well let me know, shirts are buy one, get one half off."

The problem with weekends is that they are long and boring. You're not doing real work. It's just talking to people, walking around and grabbing things off high shelves. Getting a paycheck feels like cheating. If I caught shoplifters I wouldn't feel so bad, but I don't so I feel like my job on the weekends could be done by an iPhone taped to a mannequin.

Two black teenage girls with large bags from Body Central come in the store.

"Hey guys, how are you doing? Anything I can help you find? Okay, well let me know, shirts are buy one, get one half off."

"Excuse me?" The family waves me over to the lights. Across the store Patrick flirts with a boy in a Bright Eyes shirt, even though the lights are in the middle of the store and therefore in his area I help the family and try to keep an eye out.

"Does this one follow along with the music?" the husband asks me.

"No, actually that would be this one," I say, pointing out another box that says Four Color Dome Light! Follows The MUSIC on the top shelf, almost the same as the other dome but $30 more.

"Why so much?"

His daughter's ice cream finally drips on the ground.

"Sound activated and one more color."

"Can I take a look?"

I get a ladder from the back and show him. He likes it and I upsell the mom another shirt and cash them out for $150. At this point Britt abandons the back and starts walking around, acting all managerial. She passes by Patrick and his newest conversation. I head back up to the front.

"Hey guys, how are you doing? Anything I can help you find? Okay, well let me know, shirts are buy one, get one half off."

There are still eight speakers in the stack.

One of the black teenagers fingers some yoga pants. I turn to look at her and when I look back there are only seven speakers in the stack. Britt appears.

"Where'd the other one go?" she asks.

The other girl makes a break for it but Britt yells "Hey!" and she comes back in the store, the outline of the speaker visible through the bag.

# CHAPTER 22

I'm smoking by the maintenance corridor and reading a Lady Gaga thinkpiece on my phone when Kyle comes out the service door from wherever he was floating around in the mall, waiting for me to get off. He spots me and folds his long denim-clad legs next to me, lights a Newport. "How's it in there?"

"Britt caught somebody," I say.

He laughs. "Good." He exhales and ashes with a graceful flick. "What'd they take?"

"Speakers."

"So stupid. My mom used to work Loss Prevention, and the shit people would steal. I'd go along with her. I'd see people try to grab earrings, like $10 earrings, and I'd be like, girl. You crazy. Crazy."

They took her out in cuffs, crying, one big white hand attached to an APD uniform clamped on the dark skin of her upper arm. Past the families, the teenagers looking at the new industrial bars, past Great American Cookie and the little kids covered in chocolate, through the double doors of the south entrance and into a waiting cop car and on to every black person's second biggest fear besides lying on cold asphalt. And even though I wish I had caught her so I could make myself look better in Britt's eyes, some part of me wishes that she'd gotten away with it, that she wouldn't have to sit in a cell over some $40 speakers.

"Yeah. How you been?"

"Tired. Sick of being short staffed. I wish she would just hire someone already." He picks at his jeans. "My dad called me just now."

There's so many things I could say, but I can't pick one because I'm not sure how personal I should be with my employee in a situation like this. But I want to be liked, I want to be a boss that is liked that subordinates actually want to talk to.

"Is it going to be alright?"

"I'm not sure. He doesn't like me partying. Doesn't like me wanting to go to beauty school, for sure. I don't think he'd give a shit if I'd just work in a factory."

"I should have dropped out like you did and saved myself the time and money."

"But you didn't. And now you can do anything."

"You really believe that?"

"Of course." He stands up and shakes a bit. "If I didn't believe you could do anything, I wouldn't be here."

# CHAPTER 23

Britt takes my place by the register. "Go pick up the phone in the back. Darren wants to talk to you."

Impossible for him to do otherwise.

I sit down at the tiny desk in the back and pull that folding chair up close, delaying the conversation as long as I can. The receiver rests on the table and I pick it up, pressing it to my ear. "Hey Darren."

"Ah, yes. Vic," he says. I envy his clipped phone voice. All salt-and-pepper hair and button-down shirts. "I just wanted to talk to you about some Loss Prevention stuff, thought it might be good to review some basics, make sure everything is compliant. So why don't you just walk me through what you do on a typical day you open. Not cleaning and straightening and all that, but just with the registers."

Not what I was expecting, but okay. "Alright well, I count the drawers, make sure they're at 400 and see if I need any change. Then I grab the deposit bag, or bags I guess, and take them to the bank and drop them off and get my coins, then I come back, open the store in Paragon, and finish whatever I have to before the gate goes up."

"Hmm," he says.

"Something wrong?" I ask.

"No, nothing. That sounds right. So I just wanted to talk to you real quick about the money that went missing last week."

"Ah. Yeah. The three grand."

He pauses. "No, the ten grand."

I could just quit my job right now, find another one, change my name, use this as an excuse to find the impetus to do something else, get out of here, take a risk, make the plunge, reinvent myself, you are the architect of your future, man, this time it could be me in those cuffs, stuffed in the back of the Impala. "What?"

Darren pauses. "Britt didn't tell you?" he said in a voice that makes it clear that Britt was supposed to tell me.

"No."

"Alright. Well last Sunday, the deposit you made was just one bag. There should have been a total of three, so you know, we're investigating."

We're investigating. Like I don't know what that means. Treating me like a child, or maybe the tacit understanding is enough — "Did you steal the money, Vic?" The missing product, my constant ineptitude. It all points to me.

"Altogether, your store has experienced ten grand in cash theft over the past two months," he says. "There are no cameras in your store, right? So it's going to be difficult to figure out what happened, but we're going to do the best we can. There's a new code for the safe, just in case. I should also tell you that this is not necessarily a theft. Most of the time it's a clerical error, or it's missing. That said, don't discuss this with anyone in the store."

"Not even Patrick? I mean, he was there. Or Britt?"

"No, not even them."

If I am arrested, if I am charged. Fuck my father and his stipulations, the university won't even take me if I get into any kind of trouble. Even if I'm not convicted it won't matter, I won't be able to leave Indiana. The long gray autumn and winter stretch out before me beyond the hot nights of summer, endless cold fields of clouds and ice, and I casually realize that if I'm still here in August I'll put Henshaw's gun in my mouth.

"There was only one bag in that safe, I swear."

"No, I believe you. Like I said, we're investigating."

Only the certain knowledge that I'm innocent, that none of this was my fault lets me keep it together. I briefly consider telling Darren that it wasn't me, claiming my innocence, but I notice how he's avoided words like theft or even making any accusations at all. Desperate pleas at this point won't do anything but cast suspicion or heighten perceptions of incompetence. Keep quiet and plan my next move.

"Okay."

"So we'll be in touch," he says.

"Yeah, you have a good one. Bye."

I return to the sales floor and the registers. "Done?" Britt asks, fixing tongue rings.

# CHAPTER 24

I am 10 years old.

"Do you know how much I do for you?" My father turns the wheel towards the liquor store. "How much time I have spent on you? I am out here until 10 PM, I have work to do, I have Spencer on my ass, up my ass, trying to get me to fucking turn in this document, and I am out here, taking you to the range, trying to fix your swing, trying to teach you golf, giving up my time and letting fall apart and ruining my practice session so your stupid ungrateful ass can play pro."

"I just didn't get it."

"You didn't listen! You never listen! The dog that does not hear the call of its master is a lost dog. And that's you. You'll see. You think it's fun? You want to work 9 to 5? I have Spencer out there, on my ass, my project is falling apart, and I'm still out here in the middle of the night trying to get you a career."

"You have a good job. You drive a Lexus."

"You think I have a good job. No I don't Victor. My job suck. It suck."

He stops and buys two six-packs of Yeungling and gets

back in the car. We drive home to eat leftover melon sauce with beef in it.

"Do you want rice or eba?" he yells at me. My mother sits on the couch in silence with her arms folded.

"Speak up! I am not a mind-reader!"

I want rice but I start to cry.

"Fine. I'll just make eba." He sets a pot of water on the stove to boil and gets the garri out of the cabinet. He slams it down on the light blue countertop. "You know what. No. Suzanne. Come in here please."

My mother doesn't answer. She just stares at the soccer game on the TV that's up all the way.

"Suzanne? I called you." His voice gets louder. "Suzanne!"

She stands up and spins around. "Don't yell at me."

"Fine. Victor, come here." He stands both of us in front of him. "Stop crying. Now."

I choke back the tears but it doesn't work.

"I'm going to count to 10."

By the time he gets to 8 I manage it.

"You know how I know you aren't really crying? Because you can stop it." He takes another drink of beer. "Now, listen.

"When I was your age I didn't have anyone to give me anything. I didn't have anyone busting their ass to give me a career. My father wouldn't even let me fly a kite. Do you hear me? Look at me. I couldn't even fly a kite. That man used me as his butler. He made me scrub everything. He made me clean that entire house in Nigeria. Do I make you scrub anything? Answer me!"

"No."

"No, what? No, goat?"

"No, dad."

"When I talk to you, you answer, and it had better be 'Yes, dad,' or 'No, dad.' Now. You can't even clean your room. He made me scrub. When I was your age I would drag the furniture out of the house and scrub the floors and dust the walls. I would do all of that, every week, until I left for college. And if I didn't do it right, he would beat me. Do I beat you?"

"No, dad."

"How would you like it if I did that? If every time you mishit the ball or didn't use your hip I beat you? Standing there with a switch in my hand?"

"No, dad."

"He didn't give me anything. He gave me school and that was it. Now I have Spencer coming after me, I have VP's coming after me that want to see my ass roast like a nice, juicy roasted meat. They want to put me on the birdie boiler. Do you understand? You don't get it. You don't get what I do for you. How would you like it if all of this was gone? My ass has to go to work, fix the flowers, cut your hair, dye your mother's hair, and still come home and cook for your ungrateful, stupid, stubborn ass. You don't know how good you have it."

And he's right but I guess at the time it doesn't feel like it, because I just keep crying and crying.

"Stop crying. Do you hear me? Stop crying. Do not defy me. You're gonna find out who wears the pants in this house." He grabs my face, four fingers and a thumb digging in, and it hurts and that makes me cry more. "Stop it right now."

I look him in the eye and just start bawling.

"That's it." He throws his bottle into the trash and it breaks.

"Tunde!" my mother says.

"Shut up Suzanne. This is between me and Victor. You listen to me, you ungrateful little twit." He gets in my face and I can smell the oil from his roughly shaven face. "You stubborn little, ungrateful, fuzzy-headed twit. I am father. You will respect me. You better stop crying."

"I can't. Stop yelling at me."

"I am your father. Don't make me do something we'll both regret. So shut the fuck up with your stupid ass crying, you ungrateful twit. You don't get it do you? You think you can defy me? I brought you in. I can take you out."

We finally eat sometime around midnight. The food is delicious. Melon sauce is my favorite.

# CHAPTER 25

The towel twists and squeaks in my teeth as I scream into it, curled on the floor of my bedroom, half-naked. The screams go on and on, filling my ears but not escaping out past my lips and into the surrounding air. My abdominal muscles seize up and cramp as I curl even harder. My mind is running through images as thoughts pound in on themselves and I try to direct them elsewhere but it won't work, they won't obey me and they build why won't it stop it'll stop if I can just wait just wait a bit it will stop.

*If I get pinned for the theft I will go to prison they will take me away in cuffs and I will have a criminal record I'll never work again I'll be beaten and raped in prison they won't care no that won't happen they'll fine you and give you probation you'll lose your job and you can't go home HE won't let you in and he will berate you and beat you he will make you sit there while he lists your failings you will mention everything you remember my father lays his rifle across the bed and he'll tell you it never happened never happened never did it never happen did none of it ever happen I can't remember why can't I remember you will never leave this city you will die by the river I need a cigarette if I can get a cigarette I will be fine where are my cigarettes unball your fist where are my cigarettes no condition is permanent all will be well no condition is permanent no condition is permanent please I just need a moment if you would please just*

# CHAPTER 26

Days off are spent alone in my apartment. I was going to live with Henshaw but that fell through when he broke up with his ex. Now I'm stuck in this storage center for young bachelors and the elderly. I watch endless re-runs of *How I Met Your Mother* and *It's Always Sunny in Philadelphia* on Netflix because it kind of fools me into thinking I live with friends.

I don't even bother brushing my teeth, I just put a pan of chicken nuggets and fries in the oven and take a shower, worried that I'll burn them before I get out but not nearly enough to justify waiting. When I get out the food hasn't even browned yet, so I light up and pop a Diet Coke and turn on Netflix while endlessly flipping through my Tumblr and Facebook at alternate intervals. There's nothing new going on, just endless drama and talk about microaggressions, a couple new hashtags, so I load up Documenting Reality and I find a video of an Indian guy absentmindedly grabbing a live wire on top of a train. The screen lights up and there's an incredibly loud pop as the electricity runs through him in a massive pulse, and he slumps over, probably dead.

My phone rings, unknown number. Not thinking, I pick it up and put it on speaker.

"*Hello Mr. Adewale. I'm calling from Solutions International in regards to your account. Your total debt is now in the amount of $12,582 and if we cannot receive payment we will be forced to take other measures.*"

I hang it up, and breathe deep for a moment. I pour myself some Evan Williams in a water glass and drop ice cubes in it. I go to the bathroom and crush an Adderall on the counter and snort it with a conveniently placed straw.

When the food is done I smother it in blue cheese dressing and eat it with another Diet Coke, then I smoke another cigarette and open another can, pouring it in a glass with more bourbon. I fire up PornHub and flicked through the categories: Anal, Big Tits, Ebony, Latina, Bi. Then I start trying keywords: "pegging," "big ass Latina," "ebony fishnets," "crossdresser," "throatfucking." It isn't working for me so I plug in my external hard drive and go through my copious picture collection. I find the folder marked "yaoi" and open it.

*Yaoi* in this context is basically just Japanese gay *hentai*, or cartoon pornography. People spend a lot of time and effort on this stuff, crafting whole worlds and storylines for their characters to inhabit. Most of it is poorly drawn and not explicit, but through painstaking curation I've acquired something like 1,500 single images of sufficient quality for my needs.

The preference for *hentai* is a carryover from my earlier days of discovering my sexuality. I like androgyny, and the world of anime and manga allows for this in a way the real world, or at least the world of hyper-conventional Abboton, never will. I used to justify it by saying to myself that if I couldn't tell the gender of the people in the drawing that it wasn't gay, that I'd just been tricked by a skillful artist. This was, of course, a lie that I still tell myself. Cross-dressing and anime are often gateways for American queers to express themselves in various ways, but they can also be used to obfuscate the truth from ourselves.

My favorite picture is this one, an isolated panel from a series called *Forbidden Housekeeper*. It's delicately rendered and almost dreamy, where a masculine guy is pounding this boy in a maid costume, heels and garters and all. And he's drawn as a man, a young and feminine one but still unmistakably a man. It's this really intimate and domestic scene and you can see the bottom (*uke* in Japanese *yaoi* terms) is pretty well hung and his tongue is out, enjoying it, and the top (*seme*) has his eyes closed. The story is, they're best friends, who've known each other forever, and the maid turned out gay but his friend would only date girls. The maid, he had this crush on the other boy for years, since high school. So one day he dressed up like this, and seduced his friend who secretly wanted to fuck him, and that's how they got here. And they do this for a whole year (other stuff happens), the maid dressing up like this, until one day he couldn't take it anymore and they broke up, only to get back together later, and they lived happily ever after, and I hate myself for thinking like this. Because part of me wants someone, let's say Kyle, to give me permission to be like this. It hurts to know that I'm one indiscretion from being disowned by my homophobic parents and best friends and never being able to fuck a woman again because people in this small town don't believe in bisexuality. Men can't be queer in Indiana.

But when I live in New York, I'll be allowed to fuck anyone who will have me. Man, woman, cis, trans. On some level I know it doesn't matter to me, and it won't matter so much when I move.

After I jack off and clean up with a slightly used paper towel I realize I don't actually have anything to do. Dread sets over me at the grey expanse of void space before me, empty, crystal space-time clouded over.

I get a text from a number I don't recognize.

*Hey dude*

*Who is this*

*Wow rude. It's amory*

Amory. The woman from the food court. The girl from the balcony, when we had flowers in our hair.

*Oh hey. How's it going. Howd you get my number*

*I've had your number. We went to college together. I'm bored. Entertain me*

*What, now?*

*I get off at 9. Meet me in the mall parking lot. Or dont*

*Somebody is pushy. What makes you think I want to meet you.*

I take a nap and wake up and jack off again. In the slightly sticky aftermath it hits me how alone I am, how isolated, and panic rises that quickly gives way to low-grade depression and then nothing at all. I'm used to being alone, but it still bothers me. My mother, she still thinks I'm naturally a loner, but the truth is that I'm not. It's just that connecting with people is difficult.

Amory messaged me again. *Because I think you're pretty cool, and you probably think I am too, and we have nothing better to do. So come meet me. I'll bring you a soda.*

# CHAPTER 27

The mall closes at 9. By 9:15 the parking lot is empty. I sit on the trunk to stretch my legs and enjoy the summer weather, stretching through what feels like forever. The vast flatness ringed with anchor stores feels like forever in the hot night, especially in the stillness of quiet low humidity air.

I am only here out of curiosity, as a way to alleviate my boredom. Kyle's motives for setting us up are vague at best. Perhaps spite, or emotional masochism. I don't know what he would gain from bringing us together. I can't imagine it feels good to have someone you once lusted after be with someone else. But then again, those feelings have cooled, and they were never much of anything to start with.

I turn away from the staff access door to stare at the asphalt past my feet. Maybe if I wasn't such a wimp I would be waiting for Kyle instead.

"Hey."

I leap off the trunk, startled by the tall woman with the ratty hair holding a skateboard under her arm and a large food court cup of soda. Amory laughs, and hands me the cup.

"Boy, what are you so scared of?"

I take the cup from her. "You, actually."

She nods. "That's for both of us. You still keep booze in your car?"

I open the trunk and suck down some of the cherry Coke. The bottle of Evan Williams is a quarter full. I pour most of it into the cup and swirl it around, then take a hearty sip. Amory takes the cup from me and pulls on the straw, hard. I sit back on the trunk.

"How do you know all this about me?" I ask. "Did Kyle tell you?"

She sits on the trunk next to me without asking and pulls out a baggie. She snorts three bumps of the white powder inside off of a key and hands it to me. I do the same. "Time travel. I took a giant dose of a blue liquid some alien gave me and wound up back here."

"I'd believe that."

"He gave me your number. Said you were smitten. You probably don't realize this, but Kyle talks about you a lot. Recently, it's all been bad."

"Thank you for sharing that. Are you here on his behalf?"

"I just wanted to meet you again. To find out what kind of person you'd become. And when I got this job and saw your mug through the store window, I thought it would be good to know the other mall folk. What are you, anyway? Ethnicity wise."

I groan and shake my head. It's an endlessly fielded and always unwelcome question that anyone vaguely ambiguous must deal with on a daily basis.

"Don't worry," she says. "You tell me, and I'll tell you."

"Half-Nigerian, half-white American mutt."

"Puerto Rican. Light as fuck but I can still speak a little Spanish."

"My boss thought I was Puerto Rican."

"You don't look Puerto Rican."

"How can I look Puerto Rican? There's more than one color of Latinos in this world."

She offers me her cigarette, and I accept. "I don't know,

man. You just don't look like it." She laughs again. It's hoarse but warmly smooth. She's obviously been smoking for a while now.

"I'm not, so that makes sense. I'm not smitten by the way. Back a minute ago, when you said I was smitten. I'm not. In fact he's been saying you liked me."

"It's kind of shocking really. Considering what's between you two."

"There's nothing between us. He works for me."

She smiles and turns her head toward me in a mocking way. "You realize I don't judge, right? You and my buddy messing around doesn't bother me. I've slept with plenty of girls."

"You know they thought I was gay at Redacted? I always get that. I don't know why."

She laughs. "You don't see it? It's obvious to me."

"I'm not, you know."

"No. Don't pull that, and don't say it was just a phase or whatever. You can lie to the world, but you can't lie to me."

It's uncomfortable to have someone address it right to my face. Sometimes it feels, not like I'm leaving my body and watching myself and others, but that I'm living as a third party. It isn't because I'm depressed or bored, although I probably am, but I'm just curious because I don't understand why people spend time around each other. There are forces at play here no one understands, forces that render calculated action meaningless. To me, other people exist mostly as equations to be solved or else data to be quantified, items for my entertainment or tools for my success. I worry they are wet molds for me to press myself into.

Amory hops on the skateboard and zooms away, not too quickly. It's quieter than I expect. Everything feels a little muted. I like her. She's easy to talk to, like I've known her for years. To me it's like she has always been there, and I couldn't see her until now.

She slides by me, stops. "If you're bored, you can go." It's clear that she's teasing. She kicks the ground, takes off again.

"Is Amory your real name?" I call after her.

She laughs again. The use of nicknames and mononyms is a symptom of boredom. It is unstimulating to endlessly perform the same characters over and over, and so we make new ones. Or sometimes, new ones are given to us, as if we are on stage for an invisible and ever-present audience.

She slides by me, again. "Why are you moving to New York?"

"Hey," I say. She stops. I reach towards her and she lets me give her a kiss on the mouth.

"What's your favorite place in this city?" I ask.

# CHAPTER 28

She takes me to the largest bend in the river. The Ohio is the color of mud, and the whole reason Abboton even exists. Sometimes it's a bitter green and occasionally it's an indescribable murk, especially when it hasn't rained, but usually it's just the same dank, stagnant-smelling chocolate milk. But now, in the peace of the night, it is dark and still and vast. A coal barge floats by, blaring its horn.

"I won't be here long," she says. "I will leave as soon as I can. There's no way to pay off the bills folding shirts at a PacSun."

"Agreed," I say. We sit on a bench on the promenade, passing the whiskey bottle back and forth.

"My pops, he won't forgive me for getting a liberal arts degree. But that's what it is."

"I don't think my father understands what liberal arts is. He seems to think I'll be a journalist or a lawyer at some indeterminate point."

She shakes her head. "You'd be a terrible lawyer. You're a shitty liar."

"I'll take that as a compliment."

"Don't. The ability to lie, cheat, and steal is vital to

survival when you're a downwardly mobile cake-eater or a fucking retail manager."

Kyle's the one that started calling me cake-eater. At first I was offended, thinking it was homophobic. But he explained it to me. It meant that I was too good to eat bread like the rest of them, and instead I was fed cake as a baby. Actually, I hate sweets.

"I think Kyle is stealing from my store," I say, without thinking.

"Then he's learned more than you have."

"You aren't worried that your best friend might be in serious trouble?"

"I'm worried that his ex-boyfriend might be setting him up."

"We made out once. Don't make a big deal about it. And anyway, won't he be mad that you're hanging out with his ex-boyfriend?"

She smiles at me, and leans in, too close. "Where do you want to go now?"

"We could go to the park. Or we could go back to my place."

"Well, either way. I'm not going to fuck you. Not right now, anyway." She comes even closer. "Because you'll be gone soon. Actually, the fact that you'll be gone soon might be your most attractive feature."

JUNE

# CHAPTER 29

"Vic? Hey, Vic?" Kyle calls over to me.

I slam back to reality and realize I've been trying to put the same pair of shorts on a hanger for the past five minutes. "Yeah?"

"Could you come over here and pop my drawer? I gave the customer back the wrong change," he says, gesturing at the squat guy in a leather jacket in front of him.

I log into his register and pop the drawer. I watch Kyle's slim fingers expertly select and caress the right amount of bills, counting and counting again, depositing them with a small handful of coins into the customer's waiting hand. "Thanks, buddy," the guy says and walks away, holding a small black and white Redacted bag.

I wasn't paying attention to what Kyle was doing at the register. In the post-Darren's-phone-call world, the simple act of fixing a fucked up transaction can make me complicit in another theft. There's a certain amount of confidence you have to have with your employees. Once that's gone, the store doesn't work right anymore. I have a small, grudging sense of sympathy for how hard Britt's job must be.

"Are you okay?" Kyle asks me.

"Sure," I say, with the most managerial face and voice I can. "Everything's fine."

Kyle straightens the belt wall and I follow him with my eyes, as if I can ascertain his guilt just by looking. "Everything alright with you?" I ask.

He's quiet for a minute. "Absolutely. Everything is great."

"How's living with Henshaw?"

"Henshaw is an incredibly interesting and difficult person. And I don't get why you're friends with him."

His hair has faded, and there's something off about his makeup. He's worn that top recently, and those high-heeled sneakers. He doesn't look bad, but his hands are moving just a bit too quickly and his eyes keep darting around. I can tell he didn't shave this morning.

You stole from my store. I know it was you, and I don't know why, but you did. And you tried to pin it on me.

"To tell you the truth, I don't know, either."

"He's super weird." He finishes the belts. "You going to Chester's party?"

"I've thought about it."

"Amory will be there."

Oh, if only he knew I'd show up for him if he asked me to. "I'm sure that she wouldn't be happy to see me."

He shrugs. "I have a feeling you'd be happy to see her."

"No idea what you're implying."

When we leave for the day and I check his bag and we're both embarrassed as he pulls what looks like his whole life out for me so I can inspect it, scrutinize it, for stolen merchandise.

# CHAPTER 30

I stop by Lex's to pick him up after work and wait outside in my car, chain-smoking and dreaming of beer and the fifth of Evan Williams under my seat. Erica texts me but I ignore her. She's mad that I haven't talked to her, keeps calling me names, saying she'll stop texting but then sending another 12 hours later.

I text Henshaw but he ignores me.

Kanye West blares through my stock but actually pretty awesome speakers. Something about today really messed me up, so I'm just hoping for a better time at the party.

He comes out of the house still banging that stupid Hatchetman chain and hops in the passenger's side, bringing with him the tang of old sweat and the usual guilt and annoyance about letting this guy in my car.

"You and that Kanye," he says as he jabs the seatbelt home.

I light up another cigarette and pull away from the curb.

"He is just not that good a rapper. I just do not get why you are all about him. He's been garbage since *The College Dropout*."

I turn right, then right again to get on the highway.

"Like that's an absolutely garbage line," he says. "It's cool he got Raekwon on this track but I don't know man. Kanye West is a terrible rapper."

In response I stick my cigarette in my mouth and skip forward a few tracks. I turn my head and gave him a big *fuck off* smile as we pass a Nissan in the slow lane, orange light filling the interior.

# CHAPTER 31

The dubstep is barely audible over the sound of laughter from the street and I'm a little concerned about cops, but mostly I'm just excited because even though dubstep is still popular enough around here for there to be dubstep nights at local venues people haven't been playing it all that much anymore.

In the kitchen I make myself a bourbon and Coke, leaving my bottle on the counter because it's mostly BYOB and the place is full of cheap vodka, not to mention a keg in the middle of the kitchen. I figure (correctly) that I'll be able to get a drink later if I feel like it (and I will), and by that time drinking out of someone else's bottle won't be a faux pas. I feel awkward in my lingering sobriety, so I let Lex wander off and give dap to one of his loser friends while I find the host, this dude named Chester, who's spinning on his dinky digital turntable in one corner of the pretty big unfinished basement suffused with UV from the blacklights.

I yell hello and he nods and gives me a fist bump and I hang around for a minute until I finish my drink and then I return to the kitchen to make another one before going outside and smoking yet another cigarette, before finally just pounding my drink in frustration since I'm not drunk yet.

That means making another one and finding Lex, which I do, standing under some streamers in the basement and attempting to dance. We hang out on the porch while I open a second pack of cigarettes. Just inside the door Kyle is talking to a girl that works at Forever 21 as well as that girl whose name I couldn't remember, Amory, and I'm trying not to stare at her tight jeans and big butt and crooked smile, but Lex is talking about football (in the off-season) so I just kind of stare anyway. Henshaw finally texts me to say he won't arrive for another hour and I suck down most of my drink in frustration.

The girl from Forever 21 says, "I told my store manager she needs to fire her. Like, she's terrible at her job and if there is even one chance of her stealing from us, fire her."

"Oh totally," Kyle says, already drunk. "Fire the bitch."

"Do you know where Henshaw is?" I ask him.

"Henshaw had to go take care of business. He had to get that money, babe." He gives me an unsolicited hug.

"What the fuck are you talking about?"

"You don't know. Don't worry about Henshaw. He's got his shit on lock."

"You're crazy."

"We're all crazy. It's Abboton, baby. This whole town is fucking sick."

This guy with tattoos on his knuckles comes up and starts talking to Lex and I'm getting sick of hearing it so I in turn find a guy I know who's in a metal band and we talk about The Faceless for a minute until I wander off to refill my drink. I put too much Evan Williams in it and I'm just wishing Henshaw would show up to break the monotony. In the basement I half-heartedly kinda-sorta dance with a girl in hot-pink short shorts but neither of us are into it so I stand in the corner and text Henshaw, telling him to hurry up. I finally start to feel a little numb, which in turn alleviates some anxiety. This really drunk bro starts talking my ear off about Diplo and he's pretty funny so I don't mind that much. He points at the girl I was dancing with and says, "Damn, what an ass."

"Yeah," I say.

"You party?"

"Yeah."

So me and the frat guy do a line in the bathroom. I go outside and smoke another cigarette, unconcerned at the quickly dwindling pack. Henshaw finally shows up clutching a fifth of Jager and we high five and go inside to do another shot. The Evan Williams is gone, as I expected, so I pour myself a beer from the keg and by this point I'm kind of drunk. Amory melts back down into the basement. I want to follow but I'm not drunk enough to become what passes for charming with me, so Henshaw and I occupy a corner of the couch in the living room and watch Robot Chicken and laugh like assholes. The metal guy and his bandmate and his bandmate's sister come by and watch some TV. Henshaw and I went to one of their shows once so he shoots the shit in his usual bid for "making connections" and "expanding his social circle".

"Didn't I hit you with a flip flop that one time?" Henshaw asks the sister.

"What? I don't think so," she says, laughing.

"Yeah, you were moshing and you kept hitting me and you kicked your flip flop and I threw it back at you and it hit you in the back of the head," he says, laughing, matching her notes but a couple octaves lower.

We do more shots and I'm starting to really, truly feel it. Out of the corner of my eye I see one of the guys pass a few tightly folded dollar bills to Henshaw. I recognize what's happening but choose to ignore it.

# CHAPTER 32

"Why do you still work there?" Amory asks. We sit on the warped wood steps leading from the porch down to the walk.

"Because if I don't, my father won't help pay for me to move to New York."

"Aren't you a lucky boy," Amory says. "My family is all locked up or living in trailers. And yet you sit here and complain."

"Well yeah, but that's part of the luxury of having a job, you get to complain about it."

She nods, and stares off for a minute while I stare at the pale curve of her neck where it meets the collar of her flannel shirt and try to make things stop spinning.

"And now you're going to grad school. Last bastion of the overgrown, over-educated man child. Do you mind?"

I hand her my cigarette and she takes a deep luxurious pull and exhales, the white smoke burning my nostrils as it floats past the black sky. She shifts her weight, picking up one ass cheek then the other, and looks at me. "I shouldn't be smoking."

"Neither should I," I say.

"Ugh. It's so late. I don't know why I stay out so late. I didn't even stay out this late in college."

"It's because you're bored. No, wait," I say. "Now that you aren't in school you aren't using the part of your brain that did all the important stuff, the things you actually care about, so instead you're just kind of sitting there."

"I'm glad you're so perceptive you can diagnose my insomnia from one conversation. What important stuff are you not paying attention to while you're just sitting here?" Amory asks. She passes me back the cigarette and I take a drag and pass it back to her. "Since you're here too."

"I don't know," I say. "I should be doing something. A lot of things."

We smoke in silence for a moment, passing the one cigarette back and forth. I raise my cup. "To getting out of this shithole."

She taps mine with hers. "With any luck, after this August we'll never see each other again."

# CHAPTER 33

When I get to work the next day I run to the back and throw up in the employee toilet so hard my eyes stream tears and when I get back that "Party Hard" song by Andrew W.K. is playing.

# CHAPTER 34

"Hey guys, how are you doing? Anything I can help you find? Okay, well let me know, shirts are buy one, get one half off."

A fit looking black dude in a gray polo comes in the store. It's not so busy that we can't get projects done, so by the low standards of a good day in the retail world today is going well. I reset the Strike Zone on the hats and fill some empty spaces and start working some clearance on the Rolling Rack. Patrick watches the front and does some inane promo adjustment with the lights that Britt set out for him.

I double-check the Fiesta Folio and email, because I'm kind of compulsive like that. It eats up time when I don't have a lot to do, and it's also important to make sure that you know what's going on with your store. I check the sales numbers: disappointingly low, the usual tradeoff for a quiet low-key day. Making our daily sales goal means raises and bonuses for me and more hours for my Hosts, but I'm not as concerned with that now as I used to be.

*Wanna come by later?* Henshaw texts. *I'll have pizza. Bring booze.*

"Excuse me, I'd like to speak to the manager."

I look up, jolted and fearful. It's the gray polo guy. "That's me." The blue badge on his left breast says Abboton Police Department.

"Great, great. You're Patrick? Or no sorry, Victor. I'm Detective Powell, I'm with APD."

My abs clench as I try desperately not to shit my pants. That fear tingle you get in the legs when hit with a shock runs through my entire body, and it takes a conscious force of will not to conk out and fall to the floor.

*You're innocent. Don't give this pig anything. You're innocent.*

"Yes. Yes, I'm Victor."

"Great. I need to talk to you for just a moment. Do you have an office or something we can talk in?"

"Hey Patrick, watch the front, will you?"

I take him to the back and give him the desk chair while I dig a folding one out from under a stack of badminton sets. I sit across from him and try to figure out what to do with my hands and feet. I must not appear to be too relaxed, nor disrespectful, and above not combative. Even evasive is preferable to combative. I remember my previous interactions with police: traffic stops, shoplifters, that time one forced his way into my apartment at 11:30 at night, claiming that someone told him that there had been a hit and run and the driver had run into my place.

"What's your full name, again?"

"Victor. Victor Adewale."

"Spell that? What is that, Indian? No? What then? Ah yeah, I played baseball with a guy from Nigeria. Alright then, so. I assume you know why I'm here."

I almost answer then stop myself. "Afraid not."

"Really." He's already gotten scrappy. Cops in this town have no professional manner and only one method of interrogation. They bully. "You really have no idea."

"I'm. Well. I'm not sure."

"So you don't know about the theft that occurred. The money, taken from the safe, couple weeks ago?"

"I was told about it by my DM. District Manager."

"You were told about it. Okay so you do know." He's taking notes. "I need you to be clear here on what you do and don't know. So you were told about it. What were you told?"

"That the theft occurred."

He circulates his hand. "And?"

"That's it."

"Alright, listen to me. You're the manager here, right?"

"I'm the Assistant Manager. Britt is the Store Manager."

"Yeah, I've spoken to Britt. So I'm assuming since you're the Store Manager that you want this taken care of, and you want it done as quickly and easily as possible so you can go back to running your store, because I'm sure you have more important things to worry about. So I'm thinking, maybe you should help me out here."

"I'm afraid I've told you what I know. Which isn't anything, I'll admit."

Suddenly his body language loosens, and he adopts a more laid back demeanor. "Come on, man," he says with an incredulous grin. "Look, you ain't gotta protect anybody in here. And anything you might or might not have done, well. It'll be way better for you if we just rap right here, you feel me?"

Many people will tell you that since some black men become police officers, that means cops aren't racist. Do not believe these people. There isn't a body in the APD that I'd trust. They are instruments of the same disease that has stricken every surface of this city.

"Where'd you go to school?"

"Abboton University."

"Nice. Scholarship student."

"No. My father took out loans. I was very fortunate."

He's a little taken aback. He was going to do some kind of an angle where he played on my poverty, my resentment at growing up black and working class. I take a sick glee in watching his attempt fall short, but I can sense his mood turn.

"Well that's just grand. And I'm sure he wouldn't want to see you in any kind of trouble. The more you tell me, the less likely that is."

"Sorry, I gave you all I got."

He writes for a moment, movements restrained but physically angry. "You were here the morning of Sunday, May 19th. Is that right? That's when the incident occurred, best we can tell."

"Yes."

"Notice anything unusual?"

"I took the bags of money that were in the safe and I deposited them."

"That's it."

"That's it," and I risk volunteering a tiny amount of information. "Any discrepancy in the amount would have been noted by Home Office. I wouldn't be able to ascertain that."

He looks at me over the top of his eyes. "Neither would anyone else. Britt or anyone."

Shit. "That's right."

"So you wouldn't have gotten the money together."

"I worked a short shift the day before. I left before any deposit bags were made. So, no."

"Then who did?"

"Patrick. He and Kyle closed."

"Which means they were in the store the night before. Alone. Just the two of them."

"That's right."

"As were you the next morning. Only it was just you."

Shit shit shit shit. "Yes."

Powell sighs, and crosses his arms. "Look Victor. Is there anything you want to tell me about all of this? You don't want to help me here, that's fine. This isn't even a larceny investigation. It's just procedural stuff. This much money, it's not a lot in the big picture. I'm just trying to do my job, and you're not making it easy. So can you help me or not?"

"Sorry, officer. I've told you what I know."

He nods, incredulous and dog-faced. "Tell your pal to come back here next."

# CHAPTER 35

"Where the fuck is Kyle?" I ask.

Patrick is ringing up his last customer of the day. "I don't know."

"It's Tuesday. It's 5:30. He should have been a half an hour ago."

"I know, I know, sorry."

"Not your fault."

*Deep breath,* I tell myself. *Control yourself. Nothing you can't handle. It's not his fault, it can't be his fault, he didn't know, he made a mistake and it'll be fine. Everything will be fine.*

But I can't calm down, not really, not when faced with the prospect of closing badly yet again. Not when I've been in the store all day with Patrick, trying to tighten up my sections. It's already the end of June, Britt's vacation is coming up and I need to be ready for July 4th. There is no longer any space for me. I must make my own. Shock collar on the dancing bear says, *perform or suffer.* The cop is still waiting outside. He said he'd wait for Kyle to come in and talk to him, but that was a half hour before Kyle was a half hour late.

Patrick clocks out. He's shown up in sweatpants again.

He's wearing an American flag bar in his industrial piercing and it's hella tacky. I want to make him stay but I know I can't since there's no money in the payroll budget, and even if there was he'd flip and tell Britt, and despite having the authority and the upper hand I can't afford to not have as close to normal relations with every associate in this store.

The phone rings. "Thank you for calling Redacted, where every day is a party. This is Vic, how can I help you?"

"I got your text," Britt says. "By the way, already told you we shouldn't be texting. So tell me, what exactly is happening?"

"Kyle never showed up."

"This is ridiculous," she mutters. "Well, who's coming in? Sandy?"

"I don't know yet. I haven't had a chance to call her yet."

"Why the hell not?" she snaps.

"Because I have work to do, Britt."

"Call her. I don't want to have to come in."

*I can handle this*, I think, lying to myself. *I can run the whole store myself if I have to*, but the truth is that if Britt has to come in and close with me she'll just count the money and probably lay into me for the state of the store, tell me that we should be preparing to close from the time we open, and count it as another verbal warning. My nametag lanyard digs into my skin and pinches and for a moment it feels like a blade.

*Call Sandy.* As the phone rings out the thought floats through my internal hearing: *He should be fired.*

It isn't even clear who "he" is. Kyle has fucked me over but Patrick is worse than Kyle. Maybe I need someone to deflect blame to. Fresher meat for the mother bear. Do bears eat their dead?

*He should be fucking fired.*

"Hey Sandy."

"Vic?" She sounds a little sleepy, and I tingle with fear at the thought she might be stoned. "What's going on?"

"Look, Kyle didn't come in. If you can I could really, really use you. Please."

She lets me sweat for a minute. "Okay. I don't know what time it'll be."

"That's fine. Thanks."

In the time it takes me to shoot Britt a text (*Sandy coming sorry for text*) the store fills with customers. Around five the mall gets busier, and it stays that way almost until closing time, and of course it's a clear hot day, and of course there's even more foot traffic than usual, people flowing in and out, looking for tank tops and short shorts that say *Bitch* on the ass, yelling at me about belly rings over Morrisey's loud monotone droning, while old farts try to find Grateful Dead posters. I can't watch everyone in the store and ring out customers and get out jewelry so for all I know hundreds of dollars in stolen product is flying out of those doors, plus I keep getting stuck at the register to get rid of the line while watching potential sales wander back into the creamy beige light of the mall. Surreptitious glances to the sales screen confirm that we aren't on track to make goal for the day. People keep picking up shirts and dumping them back.

*We should all be fired.*

Sandy shows up like five feet of salvation. No instructions needed, she just grabs the folding cart and sets up by the door before going around the walls, pulling stacks upon stacks of multi-colored shirts, two overflowing black trash buckets worth that our customers have rumpled and replaced.

The phone rings again. "Thank you for calling Redacted, where every day is a party. This is Vic, how can I help you?"

"Why are you calling me?" Kyle asks.

"You get my message?"

"No, what is it?"

"Alright well look, I don't know what happened but you were scheduled to work today."

Pause. "No I wasn't. I can't work Tuesdays. I told Britt."

"I'm sorry. Well, you were scheduled. You were supposed to be here an hour ago."

"There's no way I can work today. And there's no reason I should have to work today. This is ridiculous, I don't know-"

"Okay look, I get that. But the schedule comes out two weeks in advance. If you can't make it to work, that's your problem, not mine. I'm not your babysitter. So get your shit together and get your ass in here."

"No, V." He gets loud. "Do not even start with me. You do not talk to me that way. How dare you."

The fear-colored stress in his voice leaves me no good answers. "If there was a conflict you needed to bring it up sooner. You're a no-call no-show as of now, and if you don't show up I can't guarantee you keep your job."

"This is bullshit, V."

"Hey," Powell comes up to the side of the register. "This guy coming in or not? Who are you on the phone with?"

I hesitate, then press the receiver into my chest. "It's a customer, sir. I'm sorry, I don't think he's coming in today."

The cop grunts. "Look, just tell Britt that I came in. Or you know what, I'll call her. Have a good one." Powell turns to go.

"Helloooooooooo, V," I can hear from the muffled cup of the phone.

"Look, I'm sorry," I say, and despite my frustration I really am sorry, knife-sharp rage coming up against black pity. "Sandy's here. I need to get back to work. We can talk another time."

# CHAPTER 36

*Go through the motions,* I tell myself. *Clean the store, sweep the floor, get the paperwork together. Help out the stragglers, and whatever you do don't dump on Sandy, she doesn't deserve it.*

When the voice in the back stops I stick my head through the door. Kyle's sitting, one leg over the other and dangling a camo-patterned high-heeled sneaker, in the one folding metal chair at the back desk, looking at his phone in an intentional way.

"Do you have an explanation?" I ask. "Or are you just going to blow me off?"

He doesn't say anything. Just stares at his phone and ignores me. His face screws up and prepares to cry, everything collapsing inward with explosive force, and he turns away. He looks like pounded shit. Bags under his eyes, messy hair. I can smell something on him I don't recognize but shouldn't be there.

I am angry with him for leaving me here, for locking himself up and not talking to me. For falling apart on me. But more than anything, I am scared for him.

I lean down and put a hand on his arm. "Kyle. Listen to

me. If something is going wrong, if things aren't working out, you can talk to me. I know we aren't like best friends anymore, but I can't help you if you don't talk to me. This isn't the first time you've been late, it's not the first time you've come in here looking like hell. Please say something. Because I have had a very, very bad day, and I can't do this anymore."

He won't talk. He's all bound up in a way that's clear, a way that I recognize because right now, as I tremble here, looking for workplace-appropriate words to convey this mix of rage and adoration, the real me is bound up in my skull by the last three hours.

"I'm coming by tonight," I say. "Obviously you don't have to tell me, but you can if you want to." The door swishes shut behind me and I help Sandy with the shirts.

And then I see it, when I check back at the register, check out pitiful sales and alt-tab over to the email program. A fresh one, just delivered, subject line "Upcoming Manager Visit" and I open it and skim it, only a few words hitting like errant duck-hooked golf balls. I see *New developments* and *LP manager now coming also* and *Loss prevention checkup* and *Mandatory for all Hosts on penalty of termination*. I can't quite breathe as the realization bears down on me. It can't be anyone but me. Except I know it's not, and my vision clouds as I imagine trying to find a job after this, after being branded as a thief. A voice like my father's spools through my mind: *told you so told you so told you so.*

# CHAPTER 37

Henshaw, the big meat wall, lets me in. I follow him past two old computers and the remains of an ancient HAM radio to the beat up, brown-grey-green couch, and sit down next to Lex. Half a cold, congealing, ossifying pizza in a greasy box from some local hellhole sits next to his grandfather's KA-BAR on the duct-taped coffee table. I pull a fifth of Everclear and a bottle of generic Sprite out of the plastic bags I'm holding.

"Where's Kyle?" I ask.

"Dunno," Henshaw says. "He never came home."

Kyle is the whole reason I came here with a bottle of grain alcohol to ply him with, so I can loosen his tongue and convince him that whatever is going on, I am on his side and willing to help. All I want to do is clear my name, get rid of the pink cloud of Britt-scented fear that clings to my skin.

"You mind if I hit up the Hpnotiq?" I ask. Henshaw's allowed half a bottle of the teal-colored liqueur to hang around and fester in his cabinets since his birthday in March.

"Yeah," Henshaw says. He settles into his loveseat and seems to take up the whole thing. He unpauses *Halo: Reach.* "Getting ready for *Halo 4.* Can't wait."

"Fuck the Xbox, man," Lex says. "I'm more of an old-school gamer."

I search in the kitchen for a glass but only find a mason jar, my hands shaking slightly in anticipation of the beverage to come. Something to get my mind off of work and on to anything else.

There's a small chewing sound, and I look around. Erica's near the table eating out of a box of breadsticks.

"Hey," she says.

"Oh. Hey," I say.

"You haven't been answering my text messages."

"Yeah," I say with a smile. "I've been busy, alright?"

"Okay. No need to get shitty. What's busy's name?"

"Not trying to be shitty. Sorry."

Back in the living room Henshaw kills aliens. I pour myself a drink, repeating the makeshift recipe in my head:

*1 part Everclear*

*1 ½ parts Hpnotiq*

*3 parts lemon-lime soda*

*Pour Everclear and Hpnotiq over ice. Fill with lemon-lime soda,* and down most of it in one go. Henshaw pauses the game again and Lex turns to look at me.

"Dude," Lex says.

"You alright man?" Henshaw asks.

"Fine," I say. I mix a second drink.

"What the hell is that?" Lex asks.

The words come to mind unbidden. "Blue Disaster," I say.

"Don't throw up now," Henshaw says, laughing but also looking at his couch and rug.

"Wanna smoke?" I ask him.

We light up on the porch in between big chugs of my drink. The headache starts to set in and I feel some momentary regret for my choice of after-work activity. I can feel the unbidden, unwanted anger subside and my thoughts clear enough to allow reflection and conversation.

But instead I feel my attempts at empathy or communica-
tion blocked. Whatever part of my mind that allows me to
work at Redacted also won't let me be honest or open, and I
can feel the stupid rage mixing with my concern for my job
and for Kyle, all of it rushing against a wall I shore up with
more fortifying sips of Blue Disaster.

"Why is Erica here?" I ask Henshaw.

Henshaw chews his response. "I thought it would be fun.
Bury the hatchet maybe?"

"I don't have a hatchet to bury."

"Well I do."

"Can you not do it while I'm here? I don't feel like seeing
her. I've kind of been avoiding her," I say.

"I'm trying to make a change. I've been an asshole in the
past, and I'm trying to make amends in a way."

"It just seems like you're setting us up for something."

"Are you sure you're okay?"

"No. Not really." I take out two more cigarettes. "Just
work stuff. Kyle didn't show up on time. And I think he's
going through some deep shit, and I don't know how to help
him or even if I should help him. Oh, and someone stole a
couple grand from the safe, and I'm pretty sure it's your roommate but they're going to pin it on me and I can't talk to him
about it, so I'm really not feeling much of anything right now."

"Oh man. What are you — thanks — what are you going
to do about that?"

"Does he owe you money, Henshaw? Don't fuck me on
this. Do not."

"Dude, if it was something like that, if it was that kind of a
situation, do you think I'd even let him live with me? You
think I'd let anyone owe me thousands of dollars?" He chuckles. "You need to relax. I'm your friend. If things go south I
can help you. Now what are you going to do?"

"I'm not sure yet." I lean over the porch railing. "There
was a cop in there today. I don't know what to do about it."

"Wait, a cop?"

"I wish it was possible to just fix things. Like with Kyle, or you and Erica." I gesture back towards the house. "But it isn't. I just wish they didn't have to hurt. I wish I didn't have to hurt."

"Well that's just life," Henshaw said. He put his back to the post holding up the overhang. "What's that you were saying about a cop? People don't have honor or morals anymore. They just trash everything around them. Tell me about the cop."

"I just wish they didn't have to hurt."

"You keep saying that."

# CHAPTER 38

My father, the only Nigerian, the only black member of his country club. Years I spend playing golf and swimming all summer, eating hot browns in the clubhouse, throwing my towels to the bag boys and drinking ginger ale on the patio, hating every minute of it. The white faces of teenage boys, my mud-colored, sun-warmed arms. Their looks when my pink, translucent-skinned mother picks me up from Friday Morning Nine-Hole versus how they look at me and my father.

# CHAPTER 39

"Are you listening to me?" Henshaw asks. "Hey, look at me. Jesus, you need to get it together. I don't know anything about Kyle, and I know you don't want to come work at the hospital, but I've got side work. You could work with me, for a while anyway. Are you listening to me?"

I'm sitting on the toilet in Henshaw's bathroom, convincing myself not to vomit, waiting for things to stop spinning enough for me to finish my Blue Disaster.

*When I tell my father I will never go back he rages for weeks, breaks things, screams. Gets drunk. I've thrown away the greatest gift he can give me. When I finally leave college and tell him I'm leaving his house he finally punches me, straight on. Haven't been back.*

"Where the fuck is Kyle?"

"I don't know, Vic. Dude, are you okay? How many of those have you had?"

"He's avoiding me. He's scared and he doesn't want to talk to me. I need to talk to him."

"No, you really don't. Put your phone down. Alright, I'm taking it, here. Give me that. There's nothing you can do right now. Just sit down, and maybe drink some water. We can talk to Kyle some other time, and that'll be a lot better. Do you have a cigarette?"

# CHAPTER 40

"You never listened to me," Henshaw says. We're sitting around watching *Mallrats*.

"I never listened to you because you didn't talk to me," Erica says. "You just ordered me around and made fun of me."

It occurs to me through a grain alcohol-induced haze that I am here as a buffer for Henshaw to rag on Erica, a kind of heatsink to absorb the excess emotional energy of their confrontation. Even if a confrontation wasn't guaranteed, it must have seemed likely.

"I still do that," I say, to fulfill my new role.

"Yeah, fucker, you do," she says, "but at least you're like halfway cool sometimes. Henshaw, all you do is complain and bitch me out and make fun of the things I like."

"Oh, like what?" Henshaw asks. "Like Hello Kitty? Like My Chemical Romance or whatever? Your stuff is stupid and it's bullshit and you need to grow up."

Lex is curled up and laughing so hard he can barely breathe.

Henshaw keeps going. "How old are you going to be before you get over this? There's responsibilities adults in this world need to live up to. Appropriate standards of behavior.

You don't want to be like this for the rest of your life, do you? Hanging on to all the geeks, fucking every black nerd in town, watching roller derby or whatever. I'm trying to help you here, and you won't let me."

"You're an ass," she says. "I don't make fun of you for playing games or being an EMT or whatever, or banging your skanks."

"At least I have interests besides emo music and fucking black guys."

"Hey," I say.

"Fucking jungle fever, Jesus Christ," Henshaw says. Lex just keeps busting a gut.

I stumble outside, slamming the door behind me. A half-full Bud Light sits on the porch, and I kick it. The bottle jerks out in a flat trajectory and shatters on the sidewalk. I stand looking at the brown glass remains as Erica comes up behind me.

"What is your deal?" she asks.

"I didn't mean to do that," I say.

"Well you did."

"I'm sorry about what Henshaw said in there."

She throws her arms up. "You should be mad too. Why don't you get away from those guys? What is wrong with you people?"

*My father in front of me, screaming, stamping his feet on the kitchen floor so the whole house shakes, and I can feel my own angry tears drying and re-wetting my cheeks. Then he's in the upstairs hallway, his fist flying through drywall, coming back powdered white against brown skin, hands that have washed dishes and tilled earth, scaled fish and been burned by pans in kitchens and cut by industrial equipment.*

My own hands are softer and lightly scarred from box cutters and bruised from ladders falling the wrong way. And it's all too easy to see them going through drywall too, while someone like Erica or Amory or Kyle cowers in the corner, crying in fear as the rage is passed down, like a crown, father to son.

"I'm not your toy," she says. "I'm not coming here so Henshaw can talk shit about me."

"But you're here."

"You can't treat people like this. Both of you. All of you. Y'all think you're so great because you went to college and mommy and daddy buy you shit, well guess what, you're not any better than I am. You're not that great. You can't even answer my texts."

"I don't get mad," I say, as best I can through my dry tongue and thick saliva, slurring it all together, "because I'm scared of what would happen. Because of what happened when I was young."

"Oh my god," she says. "You had it fine. Your family is rich."

*My father lays his rifle across the bed and tells my mother "One of us is going to die tonight."*

"You don't know."

# CHAPTER 41

"Listen," Henshaw tells me. It's just us now, him crouched in front of me as I sit in his recliner, out of my mind. "I know you're hurting. I get it. I'm going to make you an offer, and you're going to listen."

Once again, he's the one who isn't drunk. He will take advantage of me again, pit my wits against his, prove something after he has already gained the advantage.

"I've got this second job. It's going real well. So well in fact, that it might become my first job. And I need you to come on board with me and take on some of the excess work."

"Is this Amway?" I ask, disgusted. "Are you selling me Amway while I'm drunk?"

"It's not a pyramid scheme. It's this part-time gig with Parker Pilgrim. I know you're going to New York, and I'm sure I can't convince you not to. I'll keep trying, but you seem dead set on it. But at least let me give you some job experience and a few bucks to have in your pocket. I'm reaching out to you as a friend here."

I sway against the post on the front porch, banging my head against it. "I don't want another job. I don't want anything."

"It's part-time, my man. You need to make sacrifices if you want to make anything out of yourself. You need to work hard and apply yourself, not waste time writing poems and selling plastic dicks. Be reasonable, for once."

At this point my drinks are mostly Sprite. I slosh some into my mouth.

"By the way, you wouldn't happen to have any rich friends, would you?" he asks. "Particularly any ones you're not super concerned about losing?"

My parents are hugely in debt. They cannot afford the club, and the house, they can not afford the insurance and loans on three brand new luxury cars. They cannot sacrifice much more to my father's vanity crusade. I don't have any rich friends because I have never been able to relate to my rich friends. I have been incessantly hounded by my father, just as I am being hounded by Henshaw, to make something of myself. To not embarrass myself and my family name. Something about me is wrong. I cannot relate to the people of my own class, but then again I cannot relate to the people of my own race. I cannot relate to Henshaw, either, nor Lex. The entire city rejects me, body and soul. The dead god of this place gnaws at me and I am too stricken to move.

# CHAPTER 42

*We need to talk about your finances,* my father texts me on Father's Day, around noon. *Do you have time to connect tonight?*

It's my night off and I really, really want to lie but I can't afford to. *Yeah. Call me when you get off work.*

*No need. Meet me at the club at 6.*

*Really? The club? Can't we just talk on the phone?*

*What's wrong with the club?*

There are many things wrong with the club, and it's mere mention sends me into a panic attack as half-formed memories are activated and then shuffled away before I can dwell too much. I text back.

*See you at 6*

I decide to try and enjoy my day before then. So I pop one of my last six Adderall and drive down to the casino and park on the third level of the garage. While the hotel and convention center and restaurants and Moody's are on dry land, the actual casino itself is an old riverboat moored across the street and connected by a glass walkway. It used to be a working boat taking people up and down the river, but now it's just out there to circumvent the laws that make it illegal to smoke in public spaces.

In order to get to the casino you have to pass the upmarket steakhouse and exit through the gift shop down an escalator to the bar where Rod Stewart cover bands play on the weekend and into a gangway towards "The Boat," as it's known. What floor you arrive at depends on the water level of the river. The beige painted metal walls are lined with portraits of strung-out 40-somethings that won dollar amounts on the slots that are too high and too low at once. $7,000, $2,500, the odd $12,000. How much difference, in the long run, does that much money make in someone's life when counted in car payments and overdue bills? Looking at the hollow sockets and rictus grins, how much of that money made its way up noses and into veins?

Without the Boat, the city of Abboton would not be able to survive. There has been a pulling away by major corporations in the area as they move their operations to Mexico and China. It was once a manufacturing hub which built aircraft parts during World War II, but over the last 30-odd years we've lost, in no particular order, Zenith Electronics, Whirlpool, Alcoa, and other smaller operations. It's only Parker Pilgrim doing manufacturing on any kind of scale, and they can't keep it going alone. Corporate offices that provided white-collar work have been consolidated and moved to places like Chicago and Nashville. Laid-off workers who never bothered accruing college debt have been forced to take lower-paying manufacturing jobs, or worse, been forced into the ever-growing consortium of chain restaurants and big-box superstores which pop up every few months, creating an endless cycle of people working service jobs buying from the same people they serve, and so on down the ranks. Indiana as a state has not experienced the vicious blighting of its neighbors because the state has only one arguably major city and relies largely on agriculture, not manufacturing like Michigan or Ohio and not mining like Kentucky. But that relative prosperity can only trickle down so far. Abboton University is too small to drive employment, and while the high obesity and cancer rates keep the hospitals busy and people like Henshaw employed, it's the Boat that pays untold millions in taxes to the city.

Those taxes are then put into downtown revitalization done in an attempt to emulate the amenities of a proper city and tempt my generation into staying nearby and building it up, instead of bugging out and taking our degrees and able young bodies to New York or San Francisco where the tech jobs are plentiful and the startups run thick. It hasn't worked, but venues still open and bars add local sausage to their menus in vain hope while the Boat keeps expanding, bringing in business travelers and nearby tourists.

Inside the Boat it's all 70's chandeliers and mirrored bars and menthol smoke. The effect is a nice old hotel that's gone to shit. It would be charming were it not populated by 30-somethings rocking tall tees and tank tops staring at craps tables and slot machines with a focused and terrifying intensity. I wander over to a soda machine and fill a cup with Diet Mello Yello. Soft drinks are free.

What keeps the Boat in business isn't bored out-of-towners. It's the people who come by every month and drop their whole paycheck in one night. Lawyers and executives, sure, but also coal miners and junkies stand at blackjack and poker tables throwing down money. Waitresses gnaw at fingernails, tapping buttons on a video roulette screen, the centerpiece of the second floor. These people, the depressed, rotting masses of Abboton, are literally keeping the city alive by funding this place. It's socialism by proxy, charity with a smiling dealer, vice's own reward.

The bottom level's air is thinner and colder. No smoking, and penny slots. I slide a dollar into a machine and press buttons at random until I lose it, then slide another in. I don't know how to gamble and I don't care to learn. Gambling is an expensive habit. And since you're going to lose if you don't walk in with lots of capital and a plan, the casino and all of its glittering, clanging video machines is really just a pricey arcade.

*Why don't people go to arcades anymore?* I text Henshaw.

My phone rings.

*"Hello Mr. Adewale. I'm calling from Solutions International in regards to your account. Your total debt is now in the amount of $12,582 and if we cannot receive payment we will be forced to take other measures."*

On the roof you can really tell it's a boat. I shoot my father another text. The humidity clings to my skin and I can smell the chemical stink of the river. The "skyline" of Abboton. I count 6 office buildings, all of them shorter than the average housing project.

To walk here is to move through the shambling bones of a dead city.

# CHAPTER 43

The liquor store is selling Evan Williams for 10 bucks so I get a bottle and stash it in the trunk after taking a couple shots. Killing time, I drive to Abboton University and wander for a bit. The great thing about open college campuses is, even though you aren't totally supposed to be there no one will look at you twice if you seem like you're the right age and you're dressed in a vaguely decent way and basically look like you have money.

Capello's office door is open and he's behind his desk. I rap my fingers against the doorjamb and say, "Knock, knock," in this totally corny sitcom kind of way.

He smiles and stands up and shakes my hand. "Wow. Victor, right? How are you doing?"

"Great," I say, "really great. How's it going?"

"Teaching American Lit II for the summer, you know how it is." Capello is from River Edge, New Jersey and you can tell. "Take a seat. What are you doing now?"

I settle in and feel the familiar dread before my answer. "Managing Redacted in the mall."

He nods several times. "That's cool. Pays alright?"

"Eh, well enough."

"Any plans going forward?"

"I'll be moving to New York in a couple months. Going back to school."

"That's incredible. Where at?"

I tell him, and he nods. "That was my alma mater. I could have given you a rec letter. Well, guess you didn't need it."

There's a thrill when I tell people I'm moving. It reminds me why I'm leaving in the first place.

The campus is small enough to cross in a few minutes: library, student center, dormitories and apartments, academic buildings, field house, ancient stone administrative hall, chapel, all jammed door-to-window around and past the tiny quad and shot through with parking lots. It's a Small Liberal Arts Institution with a world-famous theatre program that is nevertheless strong in engineering and socially dominated by Greek life due to its pragmatic, conservative environs. It's a bastion of progressive thought ringed by a traditional working man's city. What's shocking isn't the few rainbow flags or the proud banners hanging from Watershed Theater proclaiming the upcoming performance of *Equus* in all its nude horse-fucking glory (never saw it), it's the nakedness of the surrounding area.

See, most college towns feature a network of pizzerias, bars, and shitty little bistros which cater to students and faculty, staffed by a cohort of rock-hard townies who resent the students and charge $20 for a gram. Not here. Within walking distance there's a single café, a slice joint that sells overpriced craft beer on tap, and a well-stocked liquor store. That's all. It's like the city rejects the university. In Abboton, the townies don't just outnumber the students 50-to-one, they outrank them by an incalculable magnitude. Students are highfalutin pissants who can't cut it in the real world, and the local businesses reflect that. As a townie, then a student, then a townie again I occupy the ignoble position of Cake-Eater. Wealthy. Local. Useless.

Later I sit in the basement meeting room of the chapel.

The fluorescent light makes me sick. At this point of my life, after years and years spent in retail stores and classrooms from early morning until late at night at times it seems there isn't any other kind of light. The blue glow of the abandoned basement comforts me even as it makes me nauseous. I put my head down on the cool laminate tabletop and close my eyes and quietly cry.

# CHAPTER 44

Before he dropped out and we stopped speaking for a while, I'd study with Kyle at least a couple days a week. We only had the one class together, but it turned out that we actually worked in complementary ways. I took detailed notes, he was good with mnemonics and visual materials. He read a lot more widely than I did. I was still stuck reading all these dead white men, but Kyle would read pamphlets and articles, all these treatises and takedowns from fringe opinions and alternative perspectives on art, culture, history. In the future what I learned from him would come back to me, but at that time I was mostly just slightly in awe, and a little insecure.

The thing about Kyle was, more than any of us he didn't belong in Abboton. He might have been brilliant enough to reach success in Chicago or LA, or maybe he just seemed more impressive by dint of being in such an unimpressive place. I still don't know. But it was undeniable that he didn't fit here. He cared too much, he knew too much, he was too much of an asshole to play sassy gay friend. I would never have admitted it, but I was obsessed with him. He made me feel clumsy by comparison, oddly shaped and ill-defined. But he never made any statement to that effect. He had other ways to give me shit.

"Have you considered not wearing a snapback?" he'd say, all the time. "Women are going to assume you don't text back."

"We both know that's not true," I'd say.

"But they don't. You should also pick one drink and stick with it. For example, I always drink vodka soda. It becomes part of your brand."

"I drink whatever fits in a red Solo cup," I said. But that was when I started drinking Evan Williams. If my brand was "human garbage" I might as well lean into it.

My other friends, Henshaw and Lex, they thought he was an insufferable, pretentious douche, a bad influence on every level.

"He wants to fuck you," Henshaw would always say. "He's a faggot. That's what they do. He's gonna turn you."

Being well read was gay. Being liberal was gay, and being a socialist was extra gay. Spending a significant amount of time on your appearance was gay, as was dressing in anything but t-shirt, jeans, or a double-breasted suit. All of my affectations, from reading books to not watching sports, all the way to listening to pop punk and new wave and my predilection for skate shoes, was considered a sign of latent homosexuality. And anything that Kyle recommended to me, Patricia Highsmith novels, salsa brands, good places to buy underwear that didn't ride up my ass, it was all met with a disapproving shake of the head from Henshaw. I was well on the way to homosexuality. It wasn't the act itself that he opposed, of course. Whatever two men did to each other under the cover of night was up to them, so long as they both enjoyed it. No, it was all the accouterment that came with faggotry. Tears, drama, emotion trumping reason. Real men took it on the chin and solved problems. Homosexuals were too busy waxing their assholes and wearing dresses to do real work.

I'd heard it all before. From my father, as he sipped

moderate glasses of brandy, one after another, killing the bottle slowly with modest pours so my mother and I wouldn't notice. He would postulate on the taxonomy of the faggot. Never the "homosexual," mind you. Faggot.

To him, it was a result of poor breeding and excess masculine libido while isolated from women. That's why priests fucked young boys, the pedophile being the cousin of the faggot. The faggot, and the lady faggot as well, represented perversion and rape, predators in gender-inappropriate clothing. They were the apotheosis of American decadence, and he was very proud that he hadn't raised one.

It is difficult to pin down exactly what about homosexuality my father disapproves of. On some level it is clear that he find the act of gay sex revolting, but it's unclear if he finds the acts themselves or the actors more offensive. Sodomy is a perversion, but any form of masculinity that deviates from his performance of it is treated as unworthy and harmful to the fabric of society. My father is a meticulous groomer who does not own a pair of blue jeans. He speculated that dirty, blue-collar masculinity is gay signaling, as is cross-dressing and effeminate mannerisms in men. He's not wrong, I suppose. Homosexuality itself is sexual activity between members of the same gender, but queerness and the manifestations thereof are top to bottom reorganizations of culture, remixes and appropriations developed separately from the cisgender heterosexual orthodoxy.

Maybe that was what I found so enthralling about Kyle. I was looking for an out, some kind of liberation from the restrictions placed upon me, and even if we only studied together it put me within proximity of a guide. He was someone from another realm whose very existence was an invitation for me to alter myself, a kind of living travel brochure.

How we stopped speaking was, we met up at the campus library to study. I don't remember what it was for. We didn't have a class together at that point. I was in my last semester, he was struggling through his second. It didn't matter though, because that day I was going to ask him to go to the gay prom.

See, every year Kentuckiana Alliance throws this gay prom for the whole city. Everyone and anyone is invited, so there's nothing wrong with a couple college kids showing up. I'd never been to prom, and I wanted him to go with me. I thought it would be cute. I graduate, and take this guy out to prom. Things would never be the same, and that's all I wanted.

Kyle came in late, clutching half of a giant iced tea and with this massive disorganized book bag slung over his shoulders. He's always been like that, with only half his shit together at any given point in time. And right away I could tell he wasn't right. There was nothing outwardly wrong about him. I'd seen his outfit before and his face was a mask as always, but there was something in the body language that indicated stress and a shrinking away, as if he wanted to be alone.

"What's wrong?" I asked him.

He plunked down the cup and threw the bag on the table with altogether too much noise, earning us a stern glance from the handful of sorority sisters at the next desk. "Hello to you as well," he said. "Nothing is wrong, why do you always assume something is wrong?"

"I'm used to being disappointed."

"How precious. It isn't a good look."

I felt myself go red, not just with humiliation but a tinge of anger. I hadn't done anything to him, so his outsized aggression grated.

He opened a book, seemingly at random, and started to read. No conversation or preamble, he just ignored me as he read, not taking notes or highlighting as I'd often implored him. I watched Kyle's hazel eyes go back and forth, slowly raking the page. I let the silence hang for a moment before I spoke again.

"You really should be highlighting."

"I knew how to do things before I met you, V. I don't need to be managed."

"I'm just trying to help."

"You're not the first person I would go to for help, but thanks I guess."

We are taught to equate conflict with progress, yet so much of conflict is meaningless. It is so often an endless grind with no purpose, especially in relationships. We fight each other, but there's no winning. Even if you win the argument, the trauma leaves scars that aren't worth the victory. And in this particular moment, I was frightened of what damage would come of this argument. So I said nothing, and let the tension balloon upwards until it was unbearable. Kyle didn't say anything, just kept reading the same page. I wanted to force him to speak. He couldn't hold it in forever. Sooner or later, he would have to tell me what was wrong, to engage with me as a human. If he was trying to use the silent treatment on me, it wouldn't work. I was raised by a former colonial subject to be stoic, to hold the stiff upper lip, and I was far too determined to allow this to break me.

"So, what are you doing around, say, the last week of June?" I asked, caving almost immediately.

Kyle shut the book and placed it on the table. "I can't do this anymore."

"You mean study? Or answer my question?"

"No, I mean I can't do this," he waved a finger back and forth between us, "anymore. I can't see you. Not like this."

"I don't get it. What did I do?"

"It's not what you did, it's what you didn't do." He raised his voice just beyond acceptable library volume and earned another glance from the sorority girls. "You haven't told anyone about us, and you still have a girlfriend. I can't be expected to stay with such a hopeless closet case."

"I don't have a girlfriend. Beth and I aren't official."

"And neither are we, but I haven't slept with anyone else in months. And we keep meeting up to 'study,' and at bars that none of your friends go to, and I always hope you'll say something but you never do. I'm tired of it, and it's over."

He had that masculine pre-cry look, and it threw me off. I was used to him being icy and detached, even when we were together.

"Well, that's what I was going to talk to you about," I began. "About us. And maybe, the possibility of us."

"And what are you going to say, V? Has it occurred to you that I might not want to carry on a secret affair like a Victorian fop in a shitty BBC movie? Or was your plan to just have me keep fucking you on the side while you went back to the country club with daddy and got married? I've been in this position too many times, V. You can't do this to me. I won't let you."

I looked down at my own books. One by one, I gathered them up and prepared to leave. Better to escape with broken dignity than to stay and be pummeled.

"You're just going to walk away."

"Sssh!" said the pinkest sorority girl.

I turned and gave a half smile before turning back. "I'm not gay, Kyle."

"You don't have to be gay." He was quieter, but more flustered. "It doesn't matter if you're gay. I'm not even sure that I'm a boy. It's not about who or what you are. It's about your refusal to admit that you're anything at all."

In hindsight, I suffered from delusion. This was fantasy, the least plausible scenario. I confused a fleeting interest, a mild perversion with genuine affection. It was a false yearning that I had fabricated, an inability to be content with my ordained place in life. My place had already been set, and there was no moving against it. To do so would be nothing less than folly.

"V?"

My vision was getting hazy. Probably tears. "You can never meet my father." My voice was getting louder. "You can never come over for Christmas. This isn't, wasn't ever, real. I'm sorry that you ever thought it was."

"Can you two do this elsewhere?" said the sorority girl.

"Eat my fucking ass," I said. I could see a librarian coming around, so I stuffed everything into my bag and slung it over my shoulder. "Or don't. It's your life."

Kyle and I shared a cigarette on the quad. It was the end of the semester, and the sunsets were the vibrant orange of chemical smog.

"Are you okay?" he asked.

In a couple weeks, I'd be through school, with a largely useless degree. The next, interminable part of my existence would begin. I had years of poverty, obscurity, and mental degradation ahead of me, and I don't just mean the Redacted stuff. But I didn't know it at the time. All I could think of was how pretty the sun looked, and how wonderful it would feel to be gone.

"Well, I just found out that I was in a relationship and got broken up with in the same conversation."

He relented enough to hug me. I leaned over and kissed his cheek.

He spent the night with me, but in the morning Kyle was gone and I didn't hear from him for the longest time. That's how he is. Without an audience, he's as silent as he can ever be. He didn't spend any time on campus anymore, and I didn't see him around. But like he said, we didn't frequent the same places. I stayed close to Lex and Henshaw, which meant sports bars, wing joints, death metal shows. There wasn't much time or space for Kyle and I to share, and once I'd sent about a dozen texts with no response I figured I better stop before I entered stalker territory.

I heard from various sources that he was alive, but that he'd dropped out and taken to working whatever paid. None of the club flyers I perused showed me his name. After graduation I made the mistake of taking the promotion at Redacted, since I was already working near full time hours and I knew most of what there was to learn in the store. We couldn't keep associates in the store to replace my spot, which led to us being continuously understaffed, and in turn led to ever more stress resting upon me.

When I finally got a call back from Kyle it was more than a year later, and right before the holiday season when. We were in the midst of Halloween and contemplating the Holiday reset, so it was around August.

I was on my lunch when I got the call. I answered with a feeble hello and cursed myself for how much my voice shook.

"I heard graduation was absolutely lit," he said, with no preamble. "I wish I could have been there."

"Well, you did drop out."

"And it was a real shame too. Maybe if I hadn't I wouldn't be unemployed."

"Yes, you would have."

"I'm calling to apologize. I was going through a lot, I had papers due and my project for Ceramics did not come together. It was rash, and I'm sorry."

"You're calling me because you want a job."

"I'm being honest, V. You don't know how many times I dialed your number and hung up."

"Put in an application and I'll push it through. You have nothing to apologize for."

I don't know if I meant it. I still don't know how I feel about Kyle, which has caused me no shortage of angst. He showed up to the interview more dressed up than I'd ever seen him. He straight up wore a blazer to interview at a shitty version of Hot Topic. I'd never seen him so butch.

"Where's your boss?" he asked.

"I'll be conducting the interview. Sandy, watch the front for me, please."

He went pale under his foundation, and opened his mouth. I didn't give him a chance to say anything, I just lead him into the back. He finally managed to speak after I motioned for him to sit in a folding chair.

"Given our history, I don't know if I can expect you to be fair."

"Don't worry about that. Why would I possibly be unfair to you?" I liked to watch him squirm. "First question: Can you give me an example of a time you went above and beyond for the sake of a customer?"

"I ordered some underwear for a girl at Forever 21. We closed in three minutes, and I had to call six different stores before finding one in Missoula that had the ones she wanted."

"Next question. Would you describe yourself more as an unknowable enigma, or just an ice queen?"

He grinned a little. "I like to think of myself more as an ice queen. Less pretentious. I do take issue with the word 'queen' however."

"Next question. Have you ever slept with anyone that works here?"

"V. Please don't do this to me. I really need this job."

"Perhaps in a causal capacity, a kind of mutually damaging long-term hook-up."

"You said you weren't angry. Did you bring me here just to humiliate me?"

"I'm not sure about that, but I am pretty sure that your answer would determine whether or not I can look over several more qualified applicants. Bear in mind, please, that I'm still not gay."

There is something very easy in being cruel. Once you can justify your actions, it's possible to do anything. Those who hurt others are often aware of their inhumanity, but are more aware of the justifications they have made for themselves. This is how the fallacious myth of the cycle of abuse perpetuates itself. I believe it is the justifications that are passed along, not some kind of abuse virus that infects the mind. It's just a matter of learning the rationale well enough to excuse your own behavior.

"No, V. I've never slept with anyone who works here."

"Make sure Britt knows that. You'll love her, she's a real

bitch." I held up my badge. "And we call people what it says on their nametag. Mine says Vic. You feel me?"

"Yeah, Vic. I get it."

"I got some paperwork for you. You got your ID on you?"

We left the backroom and went up to the register. I signed in and he handed me his license.

"Huh. So that's your real name. You're full of secrets."

He winced. "My real name is Kyle. I'll only answer to Kyle, regardless of what it says on my card. It'll say Kyle on my nametag, and you need to call people what it says on those. Is that clear?"

"Fair enough. Is this where you're staying?"

"No. I'm with a friend. For now. Kind of moving around."

"Will that affect your ability to get to work? Do you have a ride, are you nearby, are you subject to any kind of immediate threat to your physical safety?"

"I'll be fine. Once I get this job I can get an apartment. Or two jobs. I'll figure it out."

"You can always, you know."

"No, Vic. I can't stay with you. That would mean that we slept in the same place. The same bed, I assume, since you probably still sleep on that disgusting mattress on the floor. And then I wouldn't be able to work here, correct?"

I wanted to reach out and kiss his face. I wanted to beg him to take me back, to say fuck it and take that chance with him. It was inevitable that I would fall out with my father, that I would stumble from my already precarious spot and plunge even deeper into what I have always thought of as an underworld. But I didn't. I just touched his hand. He didn't pull it away.

"I'll keep my ears out, okay? No hard feelings. A new start."

He nodded. And that was that.

Later that night I went to one of Henshaw's many house-warming parties. He'd been living in his house for a few months, and he'd throw these parties nearly every weekend. It was a joke to call them housewarmings, but then again it was very real. A signifier that he had finally made it, in some limited capacity. And I spoke to him about the mortgage and how he was going to pay for it, and his entertaining the notion of getting a roommate. That's how Kyle wound up living with him and working for me.

Sometimes I expect that I should be asking him for favors, and that he would give them to me if I did ask. But there is still enough in me that is human to know that it would be monstrous to do so.

# CHAPTER 45

I get to Abboton Country Club late, of course. I am nothing if not causally disrespectful to my father, since there is no other way that I can express my rebellion. I am still dependent on this man, at least until I get out of grad school and can maybe, at last, be free of him.

The walk to the clubhouse is longer than necessary. They set it on top of a hill and the parking lot well away from it. The walkway is all done in a fake cobblestone that's meant to vaguely emulate garden paths, and it snakes downwards at a gentle angle through many unnecessary bends. And on top of that, if you just run up and down the grassy hill the attendants will reprimand you. Once is a warning, twice is a fine. Three times and they'll suspend you for a week. If you're a guest (like me) the punishment will fall on whoever invited you, and you can be banned from attending after even one infraction. So you have to do this long, meandering walk every time in full view of whoever is sitting on the patio, your every footfall scrutinized lest it come to rest off the path and onto the finely manicured lawn.

I hate this walk, and I always will. There is something humiliating in being watched. But if I want the money I need to get away from here, I need to speak to my father and placate his fears. So I put one foot in front of the other and wind my way up, careful to keep my eyes down so as not to acknowledge that I am being judged.

"Hey, Vic!"

Teddy Grynesburg, that greasy fucker. He comes down the path, jogging to meet me halfway, legs swinging in his khaki shorts. He shouldn't be here, on account of being a felon, but maybe that's just me being bitter.

When he reaches me he gives me a hug without my consent, and my body shrinks away from his.

"How's tricks?" he asks me. "You're looking good, man. Post-college life treating you well?"

I'm wearing a tattered old button-up and I've lost ten pounds from sheer stress since I graduated, so I know he's sucking up. He wants something.

"Surprised to see you here," I say.

He looks away in embarrassment. "Yeah, I fucked up real bad. But I'm a better person now."

"If I'd been caught stealing from my grandmother, my father sure as hell wouldn't invite me back. You're lucky."

"Hey, I gotta keep the old bastard happy. So I'll see you around?"

"I don't come here often."

"Well I didn't mean here." He winks. "I heard you still like to party. Was wondering if you could hook me up."

Unbidden, the image of Henshaw's face on the porch comes back to me, and I sweat cold. "Do you really think you should be hitting me up for drugs just after you get back?"

"Not saying drugs, you are. But if you do know anyone, keep me in mind, alright? Here, let me give you my number. I'm heading to a party tonight, just let me know."

There's no way I'm calling him, but it's easier to just take the number than explain why. I pop it in my phone and nod politely, then continue my purgatorial march to the clubhouse.

# CHAPTER 46

My father is already waiting for me at his favorite table, wearing a tweed jacket and a look of disapproving consternation. He is speaking to a senior member, Theodore Grynesburg, Teddy's dad, who also belongs to the SSGSS. I slide into the chair across from my father and mumble an apology in one motion.

"Ah, there he is," my father says, with a brilliant smile. "So good to see him. You remember Theo, don't you?"

I shake the other man's hand. He smiles as well. "Good to see you."

"Always a pleasure to see my son. He's why I do all of this. I'm afraid we have some things to discuss."

"I saw Teddy," I say, to buy myself some time with this false, friendly version of my father.

"Ah, Teddy. Good kid." Theo shakes his head. "Been through some stuff. I'm trying to bring him back in, you understand. Get him on the right track. Well, don't let me keep you and your old man waiting." He steps away, returning to his own table and corpse-like wife.

My father's demeanor changes immediately upon Theo's departure. "You know, I do not have an unlimited amount of time, Victor," he begins. "Why didn't you wear something decent?"

"Because I don't have anything decent. You wanted to talk about the money?"

He grunts and looks back at his menu. "I realize that you do not care for this place. But I have worked very hard to bring this to you, and I would appreciate it if you had some sense of respect when I invite you here. I raised you better than Theo's faggot son, and I'd appreciate it if you acted like it."

*Invite.* I have been forced here under veiled threat of economic manipulation. Politeness is a scourge that protects cruelty. He's weaponized codeswitching, alternating between a put-upon colonial gentleman and a fallaciously cordial buddy. I never get him at his best.

The server comes by and takes our orders. White bean and ham soup for each of us, bottle of red wine for him, large mug of Heineken for me. My father details several modifications he would like made to a dish of salmon. I don't want an entrée and so pick at random from the list of odious specials the server rattles off. My goal is to leave here as soon as possible, to inflict as little strain upon myself as I can muster. The server can sense my anxiety and bows out, letting it hang between my father and I.

"So about the money," I say.

"Always money with you, Victor." He sighs and re-folds his napkin. "I am not a bank. I am not a stone. I too have feelings and needs."

"Then how are you?" I ask, knowing the answer.

"Shit." He waves his hand, dismissing the question. He does not want to speak about how he is, but merely to bludgeon everyone with his complaints. "Enough of that. I'm not here to discuss it. I'm here to talk about your finances."

The drinks and soup arrive, far too quickly. My father throws the raw onion into the gray sludge. I poke at mine. There's no appetite here.

"How much money do you need?" he asks.

"We already went over this. Security deposit, any broker's fees, and the moving van. Also a per diem until I can find a job."

"That's not what we discussed."

"No, that is literally what we discussed. Flip to the front of the book and check. We had a deal."

"There was no deal. You told me what you wanted, and I took it under consideration. At this time, all I can give you is $1,000 towards a security deposit."

"That's not enough. That won't cover a security deposit." I'm hyperventilating and my chest feels like it's been torn open. "Have you seen New York rents? I can't swing that on my own. They're taking care of my tuition, not my rent, certainly not my food."

"Lower your voice. I'm offering you a grand. You should be grateful. Most fathers wouldn't offer this."

"Do you know how much I have in debts? Student loans, credit cards? I can't survive without your help." It burns my tongue to say it, but it's true.

"You have a job."

"And an apartment. I make 10 bucks an hour, and I'm on the verge of being fired, by the way. They all think I stole the money."

"Then you'll have to take another loan. Listen to me, Victor. There was a time when I may have given you whatever you wanted. That time has passed. You have proven yourself, time and again, to be irresponsible, reckless, and rude. If anyone had told me this is what I had to expect when I had a son, out of my life? I would never have believed them. And yet here we are."

"What did I do?"

"You didn't do anything. That's the problem, Victor. You cannot simply exist. You must strive towards something, and I see no striving in you. You're not running scared. You're not hungry."

The light flares over the course upon the middle-aged pack of members, fattened carcasses glistening under the death of June. And upon the other side, the path up to the course rests in shade, as more people crawl up and down. I want this. I want to be able to sit in judgment of others, at the pinnacle of my little world, ordering drinks and shaking my head at the tribulations of those weaker in spirit. The server takes my untouched soup and lays some kind of shank in front of me. I nearly retch.

"I would like to leave," I say.

"Your food just got here. You may be angry, but that's no need to make a scene."

"I'm not making a scene. I'm leaving." I look at my father. "You're right. I should be grateful that you've given me anything at all. Thank you for the money."

"If you want the money," he says, already cutting into his fish, "you will sit there and eat your meal."

There is nothing worse than to be under his eye. To be conflicted and hurting and to know, that any motion, any expression of my own angst will be seen as nothing less than a crime. I'm not stupid. I know I am playing the spoiled brat, petulant that my father will give less of himself than I demand. But it doesn't change how I feel. It does not assuage my fear.

I spear some of the meat and chew mechanically. It tastes like the inside of my own mouth. "Happy Father's Day."

He pulls his fish apart and scoops a bit of it into his mouth.

# CHAPTER 47

"Glad you changed your mind," Henshaw says. He lets me into the house. The TV is playing *Tango and Cash*.

"Yeah well," I say. "I need the money."

He laughs. "I got the money."

He leads me into his bedroom. I haven't been in there in a while, not that there's much to see. Just a dresser and a bed on lifts. He's kept, in some ways, the spartan lifestyle from his Marine days. Henshaw dives under the bed. His behind sticks out as he digs for something, and at last he emerges clutching a bright blue box. The Parker Pilgrim logo is printed on it in white. He opens it, pulls out an orange pill bottle, and throws it at me. I catch it. On the side it says *Parker Pilgrim Pilot Program. For Promotional Use Only. Dresdenol 100mg*

"Alright so, here's the deal," he says. "I'm basically a pharmaceutical sales rep, right? I go to these different doctor's offices, clinics, whatever, and I hand out the medications. It's mostly Dresdonol and Xidex nowadays, but there's some boner pills in here too. I tally up at the end of the month, and I get a cut of everything I sell."

"Sell?"

He smiles and taps his nose. "Here's the best part. They're

experimenting with door-to-door sales. You go to somebody's place, somebody that has a prescription for Vicodin or whatever, and you sit down and talk to them about the medications. You tell them that Dresdenol works by an entirely different chemical process than traditional opioids, and is therefore just as effective without the side effects. And better yet, with a drastically lower chance of addiction. If they're interested, you collect their consultation fee, and leave them with a free sample. They turn around, go back to the doctor, get on the prescription. Isn't this great?"

"Henshaw," I say. "You're a drug dealer."

"Weren't you listening? I'm a pharmaceutical sales rep with the Parker Pilgrim company, and part of an exciting pilot endeavor. Here, take a look."

He shoves a blue and white card into my hand. On the front it shows a happy family of four, and the words *Set Your Dreams Free* in cursive. The back is taken up with an explanation that basically scans with what he told me.

I look up at him. "How is this legal? You're selling prescription drugs out of a shoebox."

"Well, that is a bit of trouble." He looks bashful, but I can tell he's faking it. "It's kind of a conflict of interest since I'm an EMT. I'm way more likely to give someone Dresdenol or slip them some info on Xidex when I'm bringing in a suicide, so we gotta keep this between us. But besides that, we're good. Technically legal. And if not, who gives a shit. I've done worse for less. Best part is, it's not on the street yet. We set the prices."

He points at the bottle in my hand. "That's 100 pills right there. So your usual consultation fee, it'll come to about $30 a pill. I get them at about $20 a pill."

"If you have to pay them for the merchandise, how is this not the same as being a drug dealer?"

"So that means I make a nice tidy little 50% every time I head to someone's place. But you. I have a feeling you know some yuppie fucks from college who don't know what it's worth. I bet you get $50 or more. And being such a good friend, I won't make you pay upfront. You just get me back at the end. We split the difference. We all get rich."

I throw the bottle back to him. "I'm leaving."

"How are you going to pay for New York, Vic?"

"My father will help me."

"Do you know how much rent is? Do you know what it costs to eat in that city? The subway costs, Vic. And with your appetites, I foresee a lot of bar tabs in the low hundred range. I'm guessing you take out a lot from ATMs for a little late-night cocaine. I hear the coke is way better out there, actually worth buying unlike the trash they sell here."

I go back through the living room, and I put my hand on the front door handle. "Thank you for the generous offer, Shaw. I'll take out a loan, like every other grad student."

"A loan." He makes a noise of disgust. "That's what all you college boys do. You take out loans. They're going to want their money back one day, Vic. What was your major again? I don't see you having a high earnings potential. No offense. Can't you see when you're being given a lifeline? Vic? Hey, are you listening to me?"

# CHAPTER 48

We pull up to the party in Henshaw's Buick. The subdivision is considerably nicer than what I've grown accustomed to. It's set well away from the busier parts of town, to the east on some old farmland the developer must have gotten cheap in a bankruptcy proceeding. The houses are all McMansions, gaudy abominations, false petit bourgeois approximations of what actual rich people live like. The true city fathers all live in palatial homes on the north side of town, in a gated community. These ones are pale imitations. I have grown a healthy distaste for the accouterment of upper middle-class living.

This house is one of the largest on the block, festooned with unnecessary windows and sloping roofs. I turn up the radio a bit as we pass, so as to appear as trashy as possible.

Henshaw turns it back down and clucks his tongue. "Unbelievable. Well, I wouldn't mind a house like this one. Maybe on more land, though?"

"It's a piece of shit," I say. "It's falling apart as we speak."

"How do you know?"

"Because I grew up in one just like it."

I pull the pill bottle and a pack of Camels out of the glove-box from where they sit next to Henshaw's pistol, shoving them into my hoodie pockets. "Alright, be right back," I say.

He nods. "Take your time. Things go bad, just shoot me a text."

It's the usual cacophony inside. I mill about, pushing my way gently towards the kitchen. Once there I check out the bottles and feel another thrill of joy and disgust. It's all middle and top-shelf shit, because of course it is. The kids are all wearing name-brand clothes and there's a shine to their hair you don't see on broke people. I fill a red plastic cup halfway full of Johnny Walker Blue and take a big gulp as I press back into the crowd, looking for my customer.

It's amazing how we all have more in common than not. Yeah, these kids are drinking high-quality liquor and smoking medical weed trafficked in from California. But what they're doing, the gyrations and screams, the brags and makeouts, it's all the same shit. At the most basic level, there is no difference between this and any of the shitshows populated by mallrats and factory workers that I've attended. But then again, it's all the extras, the value adds, the perks that separate the rich from the poor. And once I leave this place, I will go searching for my own little baubles to hang on my miserable little existence.

I see Teddy in a corner, weaving back and forth, trying to chat up some girl. He's visibly intoxicated. I tap him on the shoulder.

"Vic!" he shouts for the second time today. "This is Vic. This is," he casts about for the girl's name, but I'm uninterested.

"Let's go someplace quiet," I say loudly, and the girl is visibly taken aback. "Not like that," I say, irritated at getting clocked.

For a moment she seems into it, but then she dips out and Teddy and I find a spare bedroom. He flops on the bed and spreads out, leather shoes still on the rug.

"Lots of people here for a Sunday," I say.

"Oh, them?" Teddy laughs. "Man, these are all college kids. They don't have anywhere to be. They don't have real jobs. Besides, my folks think I'm at bible study. Bible study, can you fucking believe it? They're so stupid."

He's a pitiful creature. I know I shouldn't judge. It's not as if I don't have a taste for chemicals. But there's something about Teddy, some basic humanity he seems to lack, that sets my teeth to grinding. He's always been like this, too, from when we would sneak off and get high and fondle each other as teens.

I pull the bottle out of my pocket and shake it. He comes to life at the rattle and does a little begging move, a little like a puppy.

"Down, boy." I say. "How many you want?"

"Can I not be excited?" He laughs. "How many you got?"

"About a hundred. Dresdenol. I got Xidex too, if you want that."

"Damn, okay." He thinks for a minute. "Gimme 20 of the blue disasters."

"Sweet action. That'll be $1,000."

He sits up. "Are you serious? I can't pay that."

I take a swig from my red plastic cup. Somehow, I hadn't anticipated a negotiation. I decide to improvise. "And if you go on the street, you don't know what you're getting. These are right from Parker Pilgrim. This is the real shit. 100 mg tablets of pure joy."

"Dude, I do not have that much money. I don't have a job yet."

"But you have an allowance. Or have things changed that much?"

"Of course I have an allowance, but I gotta make it last. I can't have my folks knowing I'm looking for pain pills."

"Technically it's an opioid-alternative analgesic. And they're damn good, too. They say it makes time flow backwards. And it's not like you have another contact around here."

He gets up, unsteady, and paces around the room. It's covered in teenage boy shit, Eminem posters and pictures of swimsuit models. Maybe the host is home from their university. Maybe this is a younger sibling. I don't give a shit. I just want my money.

"I swore I'd stay clean," Teddy says. "But life is hard, you know? And they say this stuff doesn't fuck you up as bad as the Oxys do."

"It's true," I lie.

He comes up to me slowly and runs a hand down my chest. Gets way too close. "I could pay you another way. It's been a while but I can be versatile."

"Stop it, Teddy. I need the money."

"Come on, man," he whispers. He reaches down and tries to find my bulge, and in spite of myself I can feel a growing firmness. "You know my hole is worth way more than a grand."

I grab his hand and pull it away. "I need the goddamn money, Teddy. I am getting away from this shithole, and I need the money. I can't stay here any longer. It's literally killing me. Every day is something new, some disaster I can't handle. And if I don't get out of here, if I'm still here in August, I'm going to put a gun to my head and say goodnight. So you can give me the money, or you can stop wasting my time."

He pulls away, hurt. Or maybe just drunk. He pulls a wallet out of his pants and counts out the bills, then presses them into my hand.

"I threw in an extra twenty," he says. "You look like you need it."

There are tears on my face I didn't notice crying.

On my way out I can hear someone yelling about someone drinking all the Johnny Walker. I stop by the kitchen and grab a half-full bottle of Ketel One on my way out. Henshaw is smoking a cigarette when I get back to the car. He asks if it went well, and I nod, handing him his cut. I wipe my eyes and silently stash the materials back in the glove box, and take a big pull on the Ketel One. Henshaw is happy that I procured a party favor, but he orders me to stash it under the seat, citing the likelihood of police on the road. I nod again and comply.

JULY

# CHAPTER 49

Britt and I take a seat on a bench not far from the store, across from Great American Cookie. "What's up?" she asks.

*We need to talk about the missing $10,000,* is what I want to say, but the words are crammed in my mouth and up my skull.

"We need to talk about this," I say.

"Okay. Go for it."

"Last week with Kyle, all of that," I begin, "He's having issues. I think that's clear to both of us. And what I really don't want here is an associate that's waiting to pop. Especially when you're going to be gone and it's just me, someone he doesn't seem to be grooving with at the moment."

"Do you really think you aren't grooving?" she asks, all bunched up, claws out but not really. She's draped across the bench, at ease, completely in control, watching me. "Why wouldn't you be? Have you done anything to make him feel uncomfortable?"

The non-accusation, the request for an admission of guilt. It's so obvious, and again I'm insulted at how dumb she must think I am. "I haven't. I did my job. He's due for another write-up as it is, and the fact that I was even as understanding as I was, he should be thankful for that."

"He's not getting written up."

"Okay. Can I ask why?"

"Like you said, he's going through a lot. If you're this worried, I'd suggest apologizing. Even if you aren't at fault, which you claim you aren't."

A man, blonde, cargo short-clad, thirty-something, argues with the clerk across from us, yelling about the lack of birthday cake cookies while his two small children run back and forth, and the message is clear: *you don't matter.*

"I guess that depends on how you define fault. And it also depends on which ongoing crisis we're talking about."

"I think that, whatever you think you know, you're well out of line. We are not going to talk about this, because if it's not a criminal investigation yet, it soon will be. Unless of course, there's some other error in the system to account for it. Either way, if you're really not at fault here, you shouldn't be concerned with it. Your job is not to perform investigations. That said, there's a reason you haven't been terminated yet, and I would suggest you try to keep your position."

*Quitting makes you look guilty, so you better not quit unless you want cops at your door.*

"So you're going to apologize to Kyle, you're going to leave Patrick alone, and you're going to step up. Do you understand?"

The clerk at the cookie place, she's left almost in tears, red grapefruit cheeks puffed, and the pimple-faced manager dude as come over to hand the little kids free cookies and give a voucher to the angry dad in the cargo shorts, and the message is repeated, emphasized, the constant refrain of being a servant, the message we take bitter pride in.

"You realize I want to stay with the company, right?" I lie, to try and tease out some more nuance from her. "Even if I move, I want a position elsewhere."

"I know you do, Vic," she says. "That's the only reason I'm giving you this much of a chance. I'll see you in a week. Get it together, man."

And she leaves me, hollowed out and alone, watching the little shits smear their faces with half-melted chocolate chips.

# CHAPTER 50

I go outside the mall in the middle of a particularly mindless shift to smoke. Henshaw drops off Kyle, doesn't wave. Kyle comes and sits by me to smoke too.

"How's it in there?" he asks.

"Fine," I say.

"That's cool." He takes a few drags. "I wish this weekend was over. I hate the weekends. I closed yesterday, it was awful. Shit all over the place."

"Yeah," I say.

And he looks at me, really looks at me. Dead on, none of this side-eye shit, just looks at me for a brief moment and even though I'm certain this kid is trying to get me fired I can't help but feel like he's a real human being for one second and that I'm one too, not some robot doing clockwork chores with an empty head. We're just two guys, smoking a cigarette.

"Anyway. I heard from Britt things aren't going well. They're looking to hire new people. Maybe get rid of some of us."

"I'm sorry. About last time. I was very stressed out."

He looks off into the distance. Watches some teenager spin donuts in the empty part of the lot. "It's not your fault."

"I still feel bad about it."

"You going to gay prom?"

"I thought that was in June."

"They moved it. End of the month."

"I haven't heard anything," I say. "About people being fired."

"Really? You're the assistant. Thought she'd talk to you."

"Britt doesn't talk to me about anything."

"That sucks."

I take a huge drag and let it out all slow, in a big cloud. "It absolutely does."

"You should go to the prom. I'll be there. Something amazing is going to happen. Or has already happened. I've been looking forward to it for weeks."

"Glad to see your grip on time has slipped even further."

"It's liberating, you know? To already have everything over and done with. I don't have so many questions anymore."

"I was going to ask you to go with me. That day in the library."

He stiffens.

"Man, I was so excited," I continue. "I thought we'd really blow it out, have a great time. That it would be the first night of the rest of my life. But you were right. It was never going to happen."

"You can't use people as actors in your life, V. It's inhumane."

"I'm starting to see that."

"This time next month, none of us are going to have jobs. They're going to clear out the whole store, on account of what happened."

"Stop it. You don't know that."

"I do. I know everything that's coming. You won't leave this town, and we'll never be together. There's nothing good coming to any of us."

"Shut up. I can't breathe."

"It's already done. There's no need to struggle anymore.

Just enjoy the next couple weeks. It's been a beautiful summer. Why end on a down note?"

"It's been hell. This has been the worst summer of my life. The longest summer. Fuck, I can't breathe."

"Failure isn't so bad. Everyone fails, all the time. You'll be a lot happier once you realize that none of this matters."

"I'm going inside. No, don't help me. I'll see you around, Kyle."

# CHAPTER 51

A boy travels to the palace to return the king's crown. His way is blocked at the palace walls by the first guard, who will not let him pass until the boy promises the guard half of the reward.

He continues to the inner court, where his way is blocked by the king's advisor until the boy promises the advisor half of his reward.

The king is overjoyed to have his crown back, and asks the boy what his reward will be.

Fifty lashes. To be split among the guards.

When I was young, my father would tell me how every day is for the thief, but there is one day for the victim. One moment when everything taken away is returned, and the pain caused is meted back out tenfold.

Am I the thief, or the victim?

# CHAPTER 52

It threatens to rain all day. Our sky is armored with steel gray clouds and the air thickens, carried in huge gusts that blow trash through parking lots like tumbleweeds. The smell changes: cleaner, as the chemical stink is blown away and ozone from the Great Plains swoops in to replace it. The National Weather Service issues a tornado watch until 11 pm. We ignore it, because these come weekly. If we halted all life in Southern Indiana every time a supercell threatened to come through and tear us in half, we'd be a ghost town.

"It'll just be a moment," Amory reassures me. "I just need to run back in and grab my wallet, and we can hit the bar."

We got off work and drove all the way downtown to The Pit from the east side, just to find that Amory left her wallet behind in her store. And had it been the usual bartender, that wouldn't have mattered. But they'd hired some fresh-faced young thing, and he didn't feel generous. Besides, I don't have enough money to cover both of us anyway. Whatever I'm making on the side with Henshaw is going in the bank. Not that I've heard from him since we went camping.

"Just make it fast," I say. I park the car as close to the service entrance as I can. The sky is turning purple and black as what little sunlight there was to begin with fades. "You sure you can get in? Mall is closed."

"I got a key. Don't ask how," and she winks.

I cut the engine. Fat drops of rain land on my windshield. "I'll go in with you," I say, mostly because I don't believe she has a key.

But she does, and we glide through the long concrete hallway out into the mall proper. We go by Redacted on our way around the bend and into her store. I see a light on, but turn away before I can dwell too heavily. It's bad enough that I carry that place within me after hours. To see it is torture.

We pass a security guard. He doesn't give us a second look, just goes on. Every store is closed, except for Lane Bryant which is doing an after-hours reset. Yet he didn't even ask us what we were doing there.

"I guess we look like we work in this dump," Amory says. "Or at least, you do."

"What's that supposed to mean?" I ask.

"You look like an extra from a Nirvana video."

I pull her gray sock hat off and put it on my head. "You look like a hipster."

"I'm not a hipster." She grabs it back.

"Hipster. "You're wearing Docs."

"Oh, wait."

Amory notices the display advertising the 2012 South Side Germanic Social Society's ThunderFest, sponsored by Parker Pilgrim Pharmaceuticals. She walks over to the roped off, vaguely patriotic display, and steps over the barrier. She sits sideways in an oversized red, white, and blue lawn chair. "Take a picture," she says.

Through the screen of my phone she looks carefree, limp, stretched, her twisting smile present as always. It's like she's comfortable anywhere, someone that carries a little home wherever she goes and welcomes people in based on arbitrary and arcane criteria even she doesn't know. Has she let me in? I'm subsumed, a character in her life even if I'm trapped in my mind. It's all about her and the new stasis she's imposed, a reordering of reality she likely never intended. Everything has been erased, the structures have fallen down. There's just her, reclining like Manet's Olympia in a plastic chair on plastic grass in a plastic display, framed in the glass of the iPhone.

I snap once, then twice and send them to her then sit on a little lawn ottoman thing covered in AstroTurf.

"What's the big deal about Thunder Fest, anyway?" she asks me.

"It's the biggest street fair in the Midwest," I say. "There's a boat race on the Ohio River and stuff. They close down St Joe Street downtown. Miles of food booths. The last night is actually on my birthday this year. It's terrible and I love it. Lex loves it too for different reasons. All the Juggalos do."

"What is it with you and him?" she asks.

"He's been a good friend, more or less. Gives me a place to go. Someone to talk

to."

She looks over at what was probably once a Structure. "I've had Juggalo friends."

"What did you get out of it?"

"Same thing I get out of any friendship. A sense of connection. They were people that I shared something with, on some level. I can't describe it. But you can find that sensation anywhere, and it'll like, bind you to others for better or worse."

My inability to articulate a confession continues to cause me emotional distress to the point where the need to confess has become insignificant: all that matters now is alleviating the distress, through increasingly elaborate exterior means if necessary. Further attempts at internal resolution only lead to a more acute sense of the difficulty involved with such an endeavor. This futility has become a regular and concrete aspect of my person, like fingernails, and while the idea of removing it is pleasant there is no way to do so. The combined system of my confession, the difficulty, and the distress has become its own thing, and I can't see any way to get rid of it and survive intact. Who I am and what I do is now predicated upon this sensation, this way of being, and to get rid of such a basic element would result in the collapse of my personality. In some unseen area of my mind I am dimly aware that it is connected to inherited expectations, but I don't know why I have this sensation. One day it appeared and I cannot do without it. There is something unknowable and monstrous coming that will tear it loose but I put this notion out of my mind every day so I can get up and drink coffee and smile. My mouth opens and words come out in spite of themselves but the ever-pulsing sensation, the wall, sits just behind my eyes, and I do not know what its confession contains.

"You know your friends aren't good for you, right?" Amory asks. "You're on different paths. Whatever path you're on."

"I know."

"I had to learn the hard way."

It would be better to let this place fall into disrepair. To die and be buried implies a certain finality. There is purity in death. Ruins are only more beautiful for having been lived in, for having once been used then discarded in due time. But to be forced to live, vegetative, an undead and nominally useful husk, lacks dignity. To continue onward in stubborn insistence that the markets aren't changing, that NAFTA and the tech boom aren't draining industry, is to be forced into existing as a shuffling parody of Americana.

She unlocks the roll-down gate in front of PacSun and pulls it up, slipping inside without a word. I stand outside and watch as she goes through the back door. There is no need for me to follow her back there. I've been there plenty of times before, to say hello to her, to give her a hard time about her sales or whatever feature she's putting up, to give her a surreptitious hug and kiss and grope.

My phone rings. I pick it up and wordlessly press it to my cheek.

*"Hello Mr. Adewale. I'm calling from Solutions International in regards to your account. Your total debt is now in the amount of $12,582 and if we cannot receive payment we will be forced to take other measures."*

I can't stop thinking about the light that's on in Redacted. It's an omen, and the last thing I need right now is any sign of doom. There is rain falling on the metal roof of the mall. Plinking reverberations fill the space. It only adds to the sense of foreboding I carry with me all the time. I have a difficult time trusting my emotional reads on situations because of that foreboding. How do you believe your own sense when they are always compromised by moody fear? But the light in Redacted. It's calling me.

I could work to alleviate my problems right now. Would they notice if money went missing, if I cut in there and grabbed a bag? It's close enough to the weekend that there's probably a couple bags in there. I could take one, tuck it under my shirt, then claim that I saw that the light was on and found the safe open. Nothing unusual about my fingerprints being on there, either.

It would be so easy for me to be a thief.

I leave the space in front of PacSun and cut back.

The gate to my store is unlocked. Was that my doing? Have I slipped so far into fractured consciousness that now I can't even close a store right? I pull it up and creep back towards the splash of light underneath the Danger Door. As I do, I realize that my paranoia has betrayed me again. No way there's anything wrong here. I just did a shitty close, and forgot to turn the light off. I chuckle to myself and look around. God, the place is a mess. It hurts to admit that I'm not good at my job, but it's true. I see an unfolded shirt and grab it. The front says *We Will Live Forever*. I figure I'll just drop this in the back, hit the lights, and go get drunk with Amory.

I push on the HAZMAT symbol. The door stops short and I hear Kyle say "Ouch!"

He's bent down by the safe, a scrap of paper in one hand,

peering at the numbers. We stare at each other as time stalls. His hair looks worse than ever.

I don't even have control over my body anymore. Next thing I know, my hands are wrapped around the front of his t-shirt and I'm slamming him, first into some shelves from which tumble an assortment of plastic snow globes. They bounce harmlessly off the concrete. I hold him against the wall and breathe into his face. It's been a long time since we were this close. Neither of us says anything, waiting for the other to break the silence. He's fighting to get loose, but not hard enough. This doesn't end well for anyone.

"What the fuck is wrong with you?" I ask.

"V, I was just checking to make sure the safe was closed, I swear." He's not even crying. Just relating it in a monotone, too fast, a voice that makes it clear he's rehearsed this.

"How'd you get a key?"

"Britt gave it to me. Just in case."

"She thinks I did it. Do you know that, Kyle? She thinks I did it, and now there's our District Manager coming down here with a bunch of cops to fire me and haul my ass off to jail."

He looks bored, more so than I've ever seen him. "I have bills, V. I have student loans. Not everyone has a rich daddy to bail them out."

I can hear the shuffling feet of the security guard outside, and I lower my voice. "They have forbearance, you moron. You can defer those. But this is the solution you came up with."

"What are you doing here, V?"

I haven't been this close to him in years. I can smell his overpriced body wash and the oil in his skin, and I can feel his smoothness under my wrists.

"Your solution was to sell for Henshaw. So don't give me any moral high ground." He starts struggling, for real. "This is about survival, V. Maybe not in the immediate sense, but in a long term, what-is-my-life-going-to-look-like-in-5-years-way, this is very much about survival."

I drop him, and his knees buckle when he hits the floor. He slides down and sits on the concrete. I stand with my back to him, letting the hormones pump through me. I'm half hard and ashamed of it.

He still isn't crying. His face is harder than I've ever known it. "Now what?"

My brain isn't functioning. I do the best with what I've got.

"Darren's coming next weekend," I say. "He'll know. You have until then to handle it."

I take his hand and pull him up. I hit the lights and pull him out to the front of the store, where Amory is waiting, concerned. I look down at my other hand and realize that I am still holding the shirt. I look at Kyle, then throw it over my shoulder and wordlessly close the gate.

We go down the service corridor and open the door. The rain has increased to a deluge. Lightning cracks the sky. My car is across an ocean, 50 feet away. I hear the howling of the tornado sirens.

# CHAPTER 53

"I know things are kind of weird right now, but I need a friend," Henshaw says through the phone. Can you meet me somewhere?"

"You're going to drive in this?" I say. Life might not stop when the storm hits, but it's still not a good idea to drive when there's a flash flood warning.

"There's a bullshit investigation at work. Now I know how you feel. I'm an EMT, I'm not a nurse, I'm not in and out of the pharmacy. It's total shit. Just please, can we go somewhere?"

I look over my shoulder. Amory and Kyle sit next to each other at the bar. There was no way we were going back downtown after this, so we cut through the mall back to the TGI Fridays, the one restaurant in this place. Amory banged on the door and was greeted by a girl with an undercut. They know each other. Probably biblically. My jealousy turns the sea roiling in my gut even more bitter, and I hate myself and all things masculine.

"You still there?" Henshaw asks, his voice far away and faint coming through the earpiece.

"Yeah. Hang on."

"What the fuck is wrong with you? Have you heard me at all? I'm sitting here potentially out on my ass, and you're holding out on me."

Please, let me sit here tonight. Let me wallow in despair and fear. Let me be subsumed in the sludgy horror of this town, drowned up to my eyeballs, unable to cope and loaded on substances. If I must be useless, let me be useless in peace, let me await my fate instead of rushing towards it or distracting myself by moving to and fro. Everything that will ever happen has already happened. My grave is old and I am nothing but bones, and the only difference between that me and this me is a string of unforeseeable events that I do not want to participate in. There is virtue in being passive, and comfort as well.

# CHAPTER 54

"Look at them all. I mean, just look at them." Henshaw is staring at a mixed family with three kids sitting in the restaurant part of Friday's.

"I am looking. I'm looking, Henshaw."

"These people, what good are they? I mean, do you think they have thoughts? Real actual thoughts about making things. They aren't real people. They're pigs. Sucking up all the effort of real people. It's disgusting. It's gross." He finished his beer and signaled the bartender for another. "I work hard. This 12-year-old girl came in with her skull cracked open from where her stepfather beat the shit out of her. Why do I have to share a world with these people?"

"Did she make it?"

"I don't know. How would I know that?"

He came to Friday's and met us, walked in the door sopping wet and barely acknowledged us. Just crashed himself into a booth and waited for me to come over. He has realized that it is possible to make these demands of me.

"They're out there. Milling around, buying crap with their food stamps. They sell food stamps, you know that right? Well of course you know that, you worked at Target, I bet you had them in there every fucking day, buying baby formula and Doritos with a goddam Hoosier Works card while they text their fucking dealers or whatever on iPhones. And the baby daddy is just standing there while the kids yell and scream, not doing shit, bugging me while I'm trying to do my grocery shopping."

He's my friend. My best friend. I get that. He means well, he's just frustrated by the same things that frustrate all of us. We are all part of the city we all hate, paradoxically providing the fodder for our hatred while seeking to destroy that fodder. Hate begets hate.

"Let me ask you something." He drinks more beer and holds his hands up, hesitating. "Why is it always these skinny black guys that are the baby daddy? It's always some fat white chick with a skinny black guy."

"I don't know Henshaw. I guess black guys like big asses."

"Yeah, they do. Fucking Lil' Wayne, man. Don't you feel bad watching all this shit? You're pretty smart, you look okay, don't you want things to be better? Am I the only one that sees how everything is going to shit? I gotta say, I don't approve of interracial relationships."

He's unsteady. Dangerous in a way I haven't often seen. He steals glances at Kyle, who sits next to Amory at the bar, hunched over in a Dresdenol haze.

"I was talking to my buddy about this. The kids, it confuses them. They don't know if they're black or white. Like I'm sure it even happened to you, Vic."

"It has, but that wasn't my fault. Or my parent's fault."

"But it's still a bad thing. It makes it harder to fit in. The other kids don't accept you. Like you're lucky, you're kind of light-skinned so it wouldn't be as big a deal for you. But like, if you grew up in a black neighborhood, what would that be like? It's just not right, is all I'm saying."

"All of my relationships have been interracial."

"That's different. You're mixed. You're part white, and there's less of a difference there."

"You've never met my father. He's just as 'white' as you are. He's the whitest guy I know."

"Okay so maybe that's true," Henshaw says, "But that's not true of most people. You don't get it, your family is rich. I've seen where you grew up, man. I've seen those houses, I know people from there. You can't tell me anything about these families growing up poor and shit. It's not the same down here. How exactly am I going to pay my mortgage? I ain't pulling in enough from the Parker Pilgrim gig to cover expenses. They upped the price on the back end, they're fucking all of us on it."

"Speaking of. Does Kyle owe you any money?"

"I'm starting to think you're uninterested in my concerns, old sport. I think you've gone selfish on me, when you used to be a hell of a good listener. I don't even want to think about how much money I'm in the hole for, but I guess I don't have a choice. I can't remember the last time my bank account wasn't in the negative. The faggot," he says, then lowers his voice at last. "The faggot owes me 10 grand."

"No one owes you that much money. You'd break their legs."

He chuckles. "If he wasn't your friend, I'd have done it already. But I just roughed him up a bit where the bruises won't show. Guy stuff, you understand. Between rent, bills, drugs, and gas money he is well in the hole to yours truly. I'd kick his ass out, but then I wouldn't see any of my cash."

"Look, I'd want to beat him up too, but if I hear anything more about that you and I are going to fight. No, listen to me for once. I caught him tonight, grabbing money out of my safe."

Henshaw nods, chews the information in his mind. He's gotten slow. My threat has left him bemused, and he seems to be pulling through that. "Well, does he have it now?"

"My boss thinks I'm the one stealing. The police are involved, so even if he had the money I wouldn't let him give it to you."

"Here's the thing. Say I had the money, and I didn't know where it came from. Then I found a way to make it disappear. You wouldn't be in trouble for that, would you? I get at least some of my money back, and then you turn his no good, lying, thieving ass in to the cops. He'll love prison. Big manly dudes, real thug guys, all of them looking for a piece of that ass."

"Stop it."

"Or what, Vic? What are you going to do about it? You have never had to sacrifice anything, so you can't see an opportunity when it's right there. You owe me. I took him in on your word, and now I know your word isn't shit."

For the first time in years, there is real fear in me. It makes me sharp, but I worry not sharp enough. Henshaw's face has grown red, inflamed. His eyes are blue stones of mixed rage and determination. I am starting to understand the full scope of what my best friend is capable of.

I stand, and say nothing. He calls after me, but I ignore him, and stand behind Kyle.

"Pay. We're leaving."

"What would daddy say?" Henshaw asks. "Listen, Vic. You've got two options. One, you can go back to that store, empty the safe, and we call it even. Or two, I can transfer the faggot's debt onto you, rat you out to your father, and then you can work for me to pay it off, and finally learn the value of a hard day's work."

"Why are you doing this?"

"Because I'm a businessman. And because ten grand is a lot of money."

I leap up and grab Kyle. "Let's go."

"But we just got here," he slurs. "It's already happened, you know."

"Let's give you a few days to think it over," Henshaw says.

"I'll tell you what I know," I say to Kyle. My temper is rising, anger replacing fear. "I know that you owe Shaw a hell of a lot of money, and that he's looking for a way to collect. Now, do you want to stay or not?"

Amory is alert, instantly sober in a crisis. "You can stay with me," she says, and attempts to herd him out of the place. She throws down an approximate number of bills for the many drinks we've had.

I lag behind, and pull out the last of my cash. $13. I go back to Henshaw and hold it out.

"Here. Consider it the first installment." I attempt a smile.

He looks at me. "Keep it. I'll get mine, one way or another."

I keep the aborted grin upon my face and stuff the cash into my pocket. I turn and walk away as slowly as I can, but break into a jog in the parking lot. The rain is heavier than ever, and the sirens wail through the blackened wind.

# CHAPTER 55

Kentuckiana Alliance holds gay prom at the Radisson near the regional airport every year on the third Saturday in June. This year, for unknown reasons, they moved it to July. They rent the biggest ballroom and deck it out, filling the hallways with information on safe sex and crisis centers and hotlines for suicidal kids that can't take the bullying. Every year, for I'm not sure how many years but it can't have been too many, a multicolored swath of high schoolers, college kids, and tired, worn-out, middle-aged people with partners and jobs that are too old to party packs itself into sedans and trucks and pushes its way out, all the way through the boondocks and the depopulated environs of Abboton's north side to this admittedly pretty huge hotel, a gaudy kind of 80s nightmare of glass and concrete with a big pool in the middle, on the inside under the huge glass ceiling, so that the whole lobby and courtyard area smells like chlorine bleach. It's my favorite building in the city, except it isn't in the city. It's way up on 41, outside the city limits, standing alone with a few smaller motels and gas stations and a Dairy Queen, well out north into the blasted empty space dotted with the odd small factory. Has to be, on account of the airport needing enough clear land to operate even if it is shabby and only has one bar and two gates.

I've only been once before, when I was in college. I went with my then-girlfriend Beth. We didn't dance and I barely talked to anyone and was basically stoned all night, going around the corner from the entrance to smoke weed and throwing back overpriced shots at the hotel even though it's an all-ages event and I probably shouldn't have been getting fucked up. Nobody talked to me all night. I tried not to notice Beth grinding with one of her girlfriends, but we still got into a huge fight afterwards and broke up two weeks later.

This year I show up sober, sober for the first time in a while. My suit is the same I've worn since I was 18, a nasty affair that's too small in the middle and too short in the leg.

Amory's here too. Her suit is way better than mine. She's at the bar, talking to an old lesbian couple, old school butch-femme types, one with short hair a waistcoat, the other a little black dress. I step next to them and order a beer, and they size me up before turning back to Amory. She gives me that look she sometimes does, that look I can't quite place, but the couple nod and turn away and tell her to have a good night and suddenly things start clunking into place in my head.

"They were a big fan of me," Amory says. She sips what looks like a gin and tonic. "Until you showed up."

"Sorry," I say.

"Why? It's not like I was trying to have them pick me up. I didn't want to be in the middle of their fuck sandwich."

"How drunk are you?"

"I'm not drunk." She leans against me.

"Yes you are." I drink half my beer. "You're drunk and you're gay."

"You're gay." She turns to me and looks away. "Ugh. Why."

"I don't know. Sorry."

"Stop apologizing. Kyle's looking for you."

"You look nice."

"You look like a slut."

"I'm wearing a suit."

The constant unspoken social ephemera. Everything smells like beer and chlorine and Axe body spray, except Amory who smells like something I don't know the name for, something comfortable and reassuring without being too warm or cozy. I've never noticed her smell before and I wonder idly if she always smells, or if I'm just noticing because she's wearing a guy's suit and the two conflict magnificently. People say that you have to have the right smell for the occasion and personality, that your outfit needs to match your odor and the room.

"What kind of perfume do you usually wear?"

"What, like right now?"

"No, I mean any other time than right now."

"I don't remember. Something from Target."

I can hear Lady Gaga thumping through the walls, through multiple walls separating the main ballroom and the bar, through worn-thin carpet and concrete floors, a constant pulse less like a heartbeat and more like the sound of road construction, an unwanted jackhammer pounding away for reasons known and disregarded. The endless bass reminding me once again that I should not be here, that I don't belong, taken out of time and place but not really "out" of anywhere at all. I order another beer and Amory wanders off, murmuring about having to smoke.

It's hard but I manage to mostly push her out of my mind as I walk out of the bar and past the giant pool, winding my way back through corridors to find that big main ballroom with its booming Top 40 music. I pass couples and trios and quartets, every gender and presentation in every color of the rainbow or glittering black and gold. Half of them look like high school seniors but also so many look older. Weirdos and straight girls and college kids. None of it makes sense, the sexless clumps floating back and forth, no sense of joining, the same dirty, infertile vibe of a dark bar and a sticky dancefloor.

The double doors, open. I recognize some of the party lights flying their payload around at high speed as Redacted products. Bodies moving, stupid dances, occasional grinding, and even though I'm far from the oldest here damn if I don't feel creepy and busted standing in the back while these kids have what I assume is fun. I have never found the release on the dancefloor they always say you're supposed to. No feeling of animal attraction, no wild abandon, not caring who sees or rather wanting people to see, not hiding. Maybe it's a deficiency on my part. Only the intimacy of another person being there, of me being alone and separate from others, just the two of us, gives me any kind of release or activates any kind of desire. I don't even notice asses in the grocery store anymore. It's all breaking down.

The Redacted crew aren't here, and I'm noticing how the older folks are just as uncomfortable as I am, floating around the edges and back and forth, in and out of side doors and slinking in dark corners. I need another drink, maybe a shot, and maybe a cigarette and to sleep for three days, on and off like I did the week of New Year's, trying not to cry and watching 30 Rock, hungover and eating lunch meat out of the slimy, ammonia-scented bag. I don't belong here. I'm not proud of anything, not my sexuality or my skin color and certainly not my hair, short and tangled and twisted. A black boy around my age passes me and smiles. I feel nothing. I put a cigarette in my mouth and go to find Amory.

Instead I find who I was originally looking for where I should have looked the first time, outside the front doors and under the vast overhang by the shuttle buses smoking cigarettes. Patrick, Kyle, Sandy, standing around. There is something forcing this world together, Redacted and the gay prom and the whole artificial representation of what it means to party. It isn't fun. It's a pain-absolving ritual.

I know they see me. Nothing to do now but go up to them, Hi, hello, what's up. I light the cigarette still dangling between my lips and pull. I still feel nothing.

"I can't believe you got to see them," Kyle says. "Patrick and I are getting ready to go. I can't wait."

"Yeah," Sandy says. "Wasn't really there to see them but it was cool."

"Really excited to see them," Patrick says. He's bouncing around. Excited little fucker. "They're like so cool. I always loved the first album, but now they released this one, I can't remember what it's called, and they're everywhere. Don't you just love that, when you know of a band first and they blow up? I can get kind of snobby about it, I try not to be but I can't help it sometimes, it's just how I am."

"What are you talking about," I ask.

Kyle kind of looks at me and away at the same time. "The 1975."

He's wearing a full-on fucking prom dress. His hair and face are all done up, and he doesn't look good but he looks, somehow, more alive than I've seen in weeks. He's been a ghost since Henshaw showed up at Friday's, calling off work and staying sometimes with Amory, sometimes I don't know where. And it's not like it was back then, but there is something in him now that obliterates, for the moment, so much of the angst we have been living under.

I wish we had never broken up. That we had come here, together, or better yet that we could go to some other dance in another city that doesn't hate us so much. But part of me, what's left of the part that can think, knows that it was just a college thing. Your first boyfriend is never your only one. One of many ways we are superior to the heteros.

"I love them," Patrick says. "Matty Healy, god I love him. So fucking cute." He seems kind of drunk even though he doesn't really drink.

"Yeah he's uh. He's really something," I say.

Patrick opens his mouth and then closes it. I know what he was going to say but I don't want to hear it. This is already awkward.

"Hey," Amory says behind me, holding a cigarette. "How's it going."

"Hey Amory," Kyle says.

She looks at me, eye half-closed. "You shouldn't be talking to your employees outside of work."

Patrick laughs, and I never noticed how mean his laugh sounds until now. "Your girlfriend is feisty, Vic."

"He's not my boyfriend," she says. She sees one of her friends and smiles and waves and moves away. Patrick and Sandy finish their cigarettes and wander back inside. Kyle pulls two more out of his pack and gives me one, so I sit next to him on the edge of the concrete planter he's propped up on.

"I have a joint," Kyle says.

"Okay."

We go around the side of the building towards the back, near the dumpsters. Kyle lights it up and passes and I take a shallow pull. It's shitty weed, but then I'm not looking to get too high.

"Have you spoken to Henshaw?" I ask him.

"Of all the nights, V, this is the one where I'd least like to talk about him." He pulls on the joint, hard. Not like there's enough THC in there to do anything. "I'm shocked, I really am. I assumed I'd be dead or in jail by now."

"I haven't ratted you out."

"Lingering affection? Or misguided pity?"

"Both. More of the former than the latter."

He laughs. It tinkles but is still painful. Reminds me of breaking glass. "You don't have to lie to me, Vic. I've seen the ends of your affection. How is Amory?"

"We're not a thing."

"You are. You totally are. I know what it looks like, okay? I am like, an expert in this stuff, and she wants you. Or at least you want her, and she sees it and that makes her go, huh, maybe I want him too. She would not be out here otherwise. There's nothing for her here."

"Henshaw told me you two got in a fight."

He shakes his head and tears start to form. "I wouldn't call it a fight."

"My father used to get drunk," I say, not even sure why. "Get drunk and punch walls. Never me. Well, mostly never me. Used to get drunk and yell about my clothes and my hair and my loud music. Say that America ruined me. Used to yell at the TV about faggots." I can see a way forward, and I take another hit. "I've never told anyone that."

Kyle drags again. "Yeah, you have. Every time you tell that story you say you've never told anyone, but the way you said it, you let that shit out all the time. Dads are fucked up, okay? They want you to be a man and they say they want what's best for you, but all they do is fuck you up. You're not alone. It happens to all of us."

"You never told me a word about your family. I don't know where you're from, or what you did before you appeared in that godforsaken class. If you have regrets over how our little fling went, that's on you. You didn't even give me your real name. I had to find that out after I'd already hired you. Any idea how that feels?"

He hands me back the joint and winces. "My grandmother's name was Kyle."

I stop with the pot halfway to my lips.

"It was almost a joke," he says. "I always wanted a girl's name. But can you imagine what they'd do to me? Can you imagine what your daddy would do to someone like me?"

*My father lays his rifle across the bed and tells my mother "One of us is going to die tonight."*

"Do you know what's going to happen to us? We're going to be here forever, V. We're going to go from job to job. And me, I'll be alone. Picking over the trash people in this town, trying to find one to waste my life with. I wanted to be a goddamn curator. Now what am I?"

*We will all be alone.*

I move way too close to him, but he doesn't push me away. "I'm sorry about what I said, Kyle. About your real name."

"Everything is so fucked up," he says. His mascara is running a bit.

I'm almost touching him. He backs against the concrete wall of the hotel. "Hey. Hey, come on. We're going to be fine. Everything is going to be fine."

He's the one that kisses me, and I'm surprised. His mouth is wetter than I'd expect based on how much he's smoked. It's only a second, and he pulls away, and looks down.

"We shouldn't even be here right now."

He makes a move to leave but I grab him by the shoulders and push him against the concrete, unable to let go, unwilling to allow this to go on. I stop short of making further demands. This is as far as I will get. Here is where it all ends.

Except it doesn't. He pulls me closer and we kiss again. Then he grabs something in my trousers.

"Sometimes I miss this," he says. "Wait, it feels bumpy."

I pull the bottle out of my pocket. "Sorry to disappoint."

He laughs and takes it from me. "This is the part where it all comes together. Do you know what this does? You should ask Amory."

"So that's why she's being weird."

"Close your eyes. And open your mouth."

# CHAPTER 56

When I finally find Amory it's where I should have looked anyway, back at the bar sucking down a Long Island and talking to a drag queen about her makeup. I sit next to her and order another beer.

"Did he find you?" she asks.

"He did. I guess you two have been talking. About me."

"Dammit. He was supposed to wait for me. Oh well, I guess he wanted some alone time."

"Do you want any?" I ask, and touch my lower lip.

"You're so stupid, I love it. I already got some, man." She moans and puts her head on my shoulder. "You smell nice. I'm sorry about what I said earlier, if I sounded like a bitch."

"No. You didn't sound like a bitch."

"Okay good, 'cause I can be kind of a bitch. But fuck it, who cares." She takes a deep sniff. "You smell nice."

She does, too.

# CHAPTER 57

The chemical makeup of Dresdenol is most similar to lysergic acid diethylamide, and as such the effects are similar. I would explain in more detail but I'm afraid that's beyond my contemplation, and therefore I'll have to describe this in the uniquely casual but term-of-art heavy lingo preferred by enthusiastic substance users.

Dresdenol actually contains two drugs. One acts in a similar fashion to many antidepressants, preventing the reuptake of dopamine. The other binds to serotonin receptors and produces mild hallucinogenic effects. In small doses, it results in mild euphoria and reduced pain along with, in some patients, increased libido. In moderate doses, there is a risk of visual and auditory hallucinations — the kind of pleasant streams of light and enhanced perception of music one associates with acid trips. In large doses like the one we just took, or took that night, or perhaps have yet to take, it will result in slow breathing, sexual anhedonia, and extreme euphoria, leading to excellent dreams and an advanced risk of death. You might become so chill, your lungs stop breathing.

Or, if you have a predisposition towards depression and/or schizophrenia, your perception of time might shift, as past events flood back into your contemporaneous consciousness and things that have yet to happen stream backwards into a memory-like state. The effects are temporary, however with each use a little bit more of the warped perception remains. After roughly nine months of abuse, the patient may experience all points of time simultaneously, becoming truly unstuck from time and ascending to a state of advanced consciousness that will surely land them in a psych ward.

Kyle, he's been using this shit for eight months.

# CHAPTER 58

I'm yelling "Hurry up," towards my bathroom door because Amory is taking far too long in there. She ignores me but I can hear a gentle snort and a thump, which I take to mean that she is entertaining herself in some way. We stopped by my place to pee and take a few slugs out of whatever bottles I have in the house before we go back out into the city.

"I'm cold," Kyle says. He rubs his arms and starts rummaging in my closet.

"It's warm as shit," I say.

"You're not wearing a backless dress," he says. He bends down and pulls off his pumps. "Ugh, I did not prepare for this."

He rifles through my shirts. It would bother me that he's taking such liberties, touching all of my things, except the thought crossfades with the last times he was in here, all the moments where he did this exact same thing. It's all running together.

"It's kicking in," I say.

"Oh, you poor thing. You won't peak for a minute. God, it's a mess in here."

My mattress sits isolated on the floor atop a box spring.

Most of my clothes are strewn around in an unknowable quantum state of neither clean nor dirty, and there's more than one empty liquor bottle. I cannot remember the last time I cleaned in here.

"I guess this answers the long-standing question of what's wrong with me."

"Depression is astonishingly common. You'd know that if you ever bothered to take care of yourself." He pulls out a white shirt. On the front it says *We Will Live Forever.* "This is mine. Why do you have it?"

"Don't wear that. I took it out of the store and forgot to put it back."

"No you didn't. It's a small, and also it's got the hole in it. You kept my shirt."

I reach out and hold it in my hands. Is this mine, or is it his? Was anything ever mine at all, or have we been sharing from the very beginning?

Kyle pulls it away and slips it over his head. "Hey now. Stay with me, okay? Try to hold on to now."

I move closer and put my arms around his middle. He puts his arms around my neck and we kiss, deep, gentle. There is nothing unclean in it. It's a little bit like coming home. I can sense the want in him. There is no want in me. I desire nothing at all, besides my very deep need to rest.

Amory stomps in swinging a glowstick. "Look what I found! You gotta try this. Oh."

We break away and look at her. She seems to struggle for a moment, but then shrugs.

"It's what I expected anyway," she says.

I break away and look through my closet. I take off my suit jacket and roll up my shirt sleeves.

"Dude, you have nothing to be ashamed of," she says.

Kyle pulls an ancient pair of my hi-tops onto his feet. "It's okay, Amory," he says. "He's like this. I don't take it personally."

"Why?"

Tears form in my eyes and I clear them surreptitiously under cover of wiping my nose.

Kyle gets up and hugs me from behind. "I don't know. Why are you like this?"

*"I'm warning you for your own good," my father says. "These faggots contain an aggressive element. They'll take you by force, if they have to. Do not get involved with one. If you ever get into a situation where you room with one, don't let them stay. They are dangerous."*

"I don't want to be dangerous," I say, back in the present. "I don't like hurting anyone."

"Baby," Kyle says. He puts one hand on my cheek and strokes my bald head. "It's far too late for that."

# CHAPTER 59

There are trees on Main street and the ubiquitous orange lights have never looked brighter, big, nasty, and beautiful lighting the brick streets like the middle of the day.. Time slides, slurring, molten, cascading luxuriously over every surface, not dripping but shellacked and spread like softened butter all over everything. The barriers between things are wearing thin like they have been for weeks now. It all finally starts to run together beautifully, moment to moment spread and interlocking. If I can just reach my hand out maybe I can almost touch it.

And it could be any night, one dry summer night after another stamped out one after the other, each identical yet impregnated with meaning created and attributed by the participant.

"There is something else here," I say.

"Yeah," she says. "It's everywhere. It's always here."

"Are we going to The Pit?"

"Yes. We're going to The Pit."

"God, you guys are disgusting," Kyle says from the backseat. He's not as high as we are, months of use cascading towards a greater tolerance and inevitable permanent alteration of his brain chemistry. "Keep it together, babies."

Amory is very beautiful but I never noticed this before because she's so far away. Does she dye her hair, or is it really that black? She shaves all of her pubic hair because she likes the way it looks, but she almost never shaves her armpits. What is her hometown like, and what did she study in college? When she laughs it sounds like carpentry.

*I remember playing on the public course back home with my dad, teeing off on number eight. I can smell burning charcoal. He looks so young, and he looks so happy even though he's having a bad round.*

In 2002 Abboton decided it was time for a change, for a new entertainment district to revitalize the old downtown and draw people back from the endless suburban sprawl. That's when they redid the sidewalks and the cobblestone and planted the trees and the new lights and made it all gorgeous. But the businesses wouldn't stick. They don't like anything too fancy. People always complaining there's nothing to do around here. Well, we got a museum don't we? And a library, and a few parks.

"I've never been to the museum," I say.

"Me neither. What would you expect, anyway? We should go sometime."

"We should have gone today."

How much did I miss, staying inside, masturbating to high-speed internet porn, trolling 4chan, refreshing MySpace. I wanted death metal and graffiti, I wanted that fringe hanging over my eyes. But I have kinky hair, nappy hair, *fuck my hair,* not pretty white boy hair, Kyle hair. I should cut it all off. I am Victor not Vic, VICTOR ADEWALE in all caps spaced out drawn across the sky in constellation lights, fuck who's watching.

*Every day feels like dying.*

Kyle isn't wearing his seatbelt so he sits up and drapes his arms around my neck and starts murmuring poetry which is just so English major I slap him on the cheek and tell him to stop and he laughs and reaches to the radio and turns it up. If it's clinical depression I'll need medication, but I don't want to go on medication.

"We're here," she says. "Hey. Stay with me," and she laughs like sandpaper again. "You alright?"

"Yeah."

We came here for karaoke like we always do because I like to sing and she likes to watch, to mock and gently needle. The Pit smells like The Pit the way good sex smells like sex. I know she smokes Marlboro Lights because I steal them all the time, sometimes without asking her and whenever she catches me she says "Are you going to buy me a new pack?" but then sometimes I actually do buy her a new pack.

*My father used to smile. Another summer night, years ago. He stopped by that ice cream place that always had the line that went on forever. It was absolutely worth it because it was just that good.*

"You have to sing," Amory says. She pours me a beer. It's Blue Moon. That's her favorite, I think. Not really fancy but not really trash. Just like us.

"I really want to. I don't know what though."

"You should do Kanye West. Or no, do The Cure. Or Depeche Mode, you always sing 'Enjoy The Silence'"

"Do I?"

"Yes, you do. Or that one Rush song you made me listen to. Or no, you should do 'Thrash Unreal.'"

"I didn't know you liked that song."

"It was always my song back home. You shouldn't interrogate Kyle, okay? I didn't buy this stuff so you could scare him while he's high."

"I seriously didn't know you liked that song."

"Victor."

I haven't been listening to her this whole time.

The man on the stage is singing something and I think it's Chevelle, slow and interminable but it sounds wonderful nonetheless. The notes sparkle and fall, effervescent, through my ears and onto my mind, splashing. My thoughts fracture and split along unknowable paths, ley lines out through my feet and all around, the world made and unmade each breath as I head towards something else. Amory has gone somewhere.

"Hey," Kyle says. He puts an arm around me and brings my face close to his. I kiss him deeply.

*My family used to smile, and laugh. We used to eat together and argue with good humor. What would they say about you, Victor? If they could see you now. Not your mother and father as they are now. Mom and Dad from back then.*

"I signed you up," Amory says. "You're doing 'Thrash Unreal.'" If she saw us kissing, she doesn't care.

The man on the stage singing this time, he's doing "Bonfire" by Gambino and he's wearing all black, brown skinned and shaved clean. I can see his girlfriend, short blonde hair and a big laughing mouth and puffy cheeks, dancing along. And that could be us, if I had been paying attention. If only I didn't treat people like shit. A little black dude is literally hanging off the top of the bar, pumping his fist. When the kid on stage is done he gets off the stage and gives the woman the biggest hug I've ever seen, picking her up. They kiss, and she hands him his drink and it crossfades for a second and it really is me and Kyle, or maybe Amory, standing there, embracing. The DJ calls my name.

My voice booms and I don't recognize it. The backing track is too loud, but that's great because I have to scream over it, like everything in me and outside me is tearing. I'm not a good singer anyway, but I fucking love this song and it makes me want to cry every time I hear it. But I don't cry, I just keep going, louder and louder, straining over the sound and not caring if anyone else enjoys it, eyes closed because I know all the words. I hear it all the time in [redacted] but now I'm singing it for real, and I know Kyle and Amory are smiling in the back.

*"We have to move," Dad says. "But don't worry. The weather is better anyway. It'll be fine. And maybe it'll be good for us."*

*But it wasn't good for us, was it Dad? It ruined everything. I became one of them, I became a Hoosier. I became bovine and complacent, and you stopped smiling. I started smoking weed and playing my guitar. Your face etched itself into me permanently scowled. There was only the constant noise of your screams and my mother's tears, and you became my father, passing the crown of tears down onto me.*

We sit outside on the patio, covered and set back from the street, smoking cigarettes. Amory is speaking but it's getting harder to follow and that makes me angry because I want to hear her. Kyle is lethargic but still mostly with it, fetal in the deck chair, his liquid skirt trailing over the edge. I stroke his head and he swats my hand away.

"Don't fuck with my hair."

"It's a mess."

"Why are you so mean? You're always so mean." But then he tilts his head back towards me and lets me softly muss it.

"It's how I was raised. My household was always full of swearing."

"Always talking about your family."

Amory lights one cigarette with the end of another and I realize that she's enjoying this, amused by our sudden physical intimacy. But it was always going to be like this.

"And that's why we're like this, isn't it?" she says. "All of us, crawling around, so insignificant, except for the lives in our heads. 'I could be bound in a nutshell, and count myself a king of infinite space.'" She waves her cigarette out towards the street, "Living their own inner life, king of their own space. And each just as interesting and varied as the next, but never respected. And that's why we're like this. Disrespected. And hurting."

Her eyes are blue. I never noticed that before. And so are the little plugs in her ears, acrylic blue the same exact shade as her eyes. And so is the little stud in her nose. Each point drawing itself closer and closer, to the center of her face, to the center of my universe at this moment. I reach out and hesitate, and gently touch that spot on her nose, and she's shocked but she doesn't mind it, she laughs.

"You sure you're okay?" she asks.

"Yeah."

She tells us about her family. About her hometown, how she came here to get away but was so disappointed in it, this place that was supposed to be bigger and better but was just bigger. The light is so thick I can practically feel them all over my hands and head, like I could scoop it off her face. "That's why I don't go back," she says. "It's all forward for me."

"King of infinite space," I say. "Eternally disrespected."

"Queen, I guess."

"Girls can be kings too."

"Would that make you my queen?"

"I'm the only queen here," Kyle says.

"You're crazy." She leans over. "I still like you, though."

Ever searching for something that will always find us, whether we like it or not. The future is already here.

*"I don't care what you say, Suzanne. I am the provider. No matter what you say, no matter how you feel, this is my fucking house and I will do what I want in my fucking house. I put this roof over your head, I go to work every day, so you and that brat can have food to eat. And if you want to live here, in this house, with your country club lifestyle, you will learn to leave me the fuck alone."*

*"So I have to sit here, in this house, while you go out there and fuck that whore, that fucking whore, and I just have to take it because you can do what you want. One day I will be gone."*

*And I can't block it out, I can't turn the music up any louder and my headphones are broken. I have to listen.*

*"Go then. See what changes. My life will go on with or without you. I am willing to take care of you, but you have to let me work and you have to leave me the fuck alone."*

*"You and your women."*

*"Here we go, always me and my women. What women, Suzanne? You're crazy."* He goes into their bedroom and into their closet. *"I cannot live like this. I will not be treated this way, I will not be accused of something I haven't done. First from my father, now from you, after everything I have done for you. I built this household with my blood and sweat, and I will not have you destroy it. I will not live like this."*

*I poke my head around the corner into their room and see my mother's back in its cardigan, set hard against him, her rage and hurt so intense it has mass and temperature.*

*My father lays his rifle across the bed and tells my mother* *"One of us is going to die tonight."*

*I don't want to be like you. I don't want to be like you. God please, don't let me be like him.*

*My own fist flying through drywall. I forgot about that. Did they love each other too, when they were my age?*

"Let's get out of here," Amory says.

# CHAPTER 60

"I needed the money, V. I was in deep with Henshaw over rent and I kept buying pills from him. Like, he gave me a discount at first but then when they started to figure out what he was doing he got all fucked up about it because he was scared he'd lose his job, right? So then he starts demanding I pay him back and I didn't know what to do. He beat me up over it once and I didn't want to call the cops because that would be my ass too."

"Hey. It's okay. I mean, it's not okay, and I'm really mad at you, but I understand."

"What about the money?"

"I'm not worried about the money. I think I'm afraid of Henshaw."

"When he gets drunk, he tells stories. Horrifying shit. He doesn't even notice anyone is there, I don't think. He just speaks into the nothing and doesn't expect a response. And he says the worst things I've ever heard, things that he did in the war, things he did after the war. Sometimes I think he's lying, that he's far too young to have done all of this. But the longer he speaks, the more I believe him. I asked him about it in the morning the first couple times. He doesn't remember saying anything at all, or maybe he does but he's lying."

"I've never been scared of him. It's very strange to be afraid of someone you used to trust."

"It's always women, too. Women and gay people, and weak men who couldn't get away from him. Sometimes he laughs, but I don't think he enjoys it. He'll sit there for hours, drinking beer, monologuing. Talking about all of the people he hates, the ones that he's glad are dead, the ones he wishes he could kill."

"Does he mention me?"

"Would you want me to tell you if he did?"

"I'm definitely afraid of him."

"They'd round up all the men in the villages, he says, and put them on trucks. They weren't supposed to touch the women, but they needed to be interrogated as well. It didn't always go well for them."

"I have a hard time believing someone like him is a homophobe. A no-shit, die hard homophobe."

"There is nothing in him but hate. This place has hollowed him out. It hollows out everyone, and it replaces their humanity with something else, something foreign and wicked. For him, it's hatred. He can't do anything but despise you and me, and himself for what he has become. And in time, it will consume him, and then all of us."

"I'm sorry about what happened to you. About what he did to you, and how I couldn't stop it."

"I'm sorry about your eye, V. You did have such pretty eyes."

"That hasn't happened yet. There is still time for us. We can be together far away from here."

"Hasn't it? My mistake. Tell me Cassandra, what do you see with your one eye? Are we happy and together? Or am I lying in a hospital bed, alone and unloved? Have you made it to the island of Manhattan, or are you still here?"

"You will never be unloved."

"You've already forgotten me. Don't apologize. I forgave you a long time ago."

# CHAPTER 61

I put on a movie and we make out on her couch while Amory takes a shower. Kyle's been crying but he's better now and I'm so out of it I'm not totally sure what's going on. He pulls at my belt buckle so I undo my pants and pull them down a bit. When she comes out, wet hair, towel, he's sucking my dick and she laughs and goes to the kitchen and drinks orange juice out of the carton. Kyle pulls his bleary head up and she comes over and kisses me on the mouth.

"You two can sleep in my bed when you're done."

I don't want her to go but she's already closing the door behind her and Kyle's gone back to it. He's really good at it and I'm feeling more torn than I expected, but then my mind goes blank and I come. Some of it gets on my shirt and he laughs.

There's almost no hair around his cock and it smells like soap and the faint masculine animal smell. It takes me longer because it has been so long, but he coaches me and he comes too.

He refuses to sleep in Amory's room but when I try to cuddle next to him he pushes me away. He just turns on some weird cartoon show.

I rinse my mouth out with Listerine in the bathroom, then get in bed with Amory. She wakes up and kisses me again, open mouth. She lets me fuck her without a condom. Kyle comes back in but he doesn't feel comfortable bottoming so he mostly just watches me give Amory head. After she falls asleep he changes his mind, but I'm spent. So I suck him off again, careful not to wake her up. He wants to leave after I make him come.

"Don't go." I say. "There's enough room in here."

Amory wakes up and she's grumpy so we all sleep in a big pile. He's gone in the morning.

# CHAPTER 62

"This is so fucked up," Amory says. "I can't believe how fucked up this is. I told you not to talk to him about this."

"I didn't." She has a very nice bed. She shares the house with three other people, but she has a very white, very soft bed. I stretch out into it and the remaining chemicals in my system make it feel like luxury. We fucked three times this morning and smoked all the rest of our cigarettes.

"If you tell Britt," she says. "you'll be selling out Kyle."

He hasn't texted either of us back. "And if I don't then I'm still suspect."

"I think you should do whatever you want."

"I'm not a rat."

She sits up and looks down at me. "You need to do something. I mean, I don't know what, but you need to do something."

"We should try to get him away from Henshaw, if we get the chance."

"Are you going to do anything to cover your ass?"

I shake my head against the pillow. "Let everything happen. It's already happened."

# CHAPTER 63

Take the cover off the driver. Palm the ball in your hand and hold the tee between your fingers. Walk to the driving area and place the ball on the tee between the markers. Step behind your ball and aim for a tree down the right side of the fairway far beyond your possible distance. Draw an imaginary line from that tree back to your ball. Take one, two, three practice swings. Step behind the ball and line your feet parallel to the imaginary line you just drew. Ground your club. Deep breath. Backswing. Downswing. Impact.

The ball flies down the fairway, and curves ever so lightly to the left, ending up only five yards to the left of the spot I'm going for.

Perfection. Or as close as I'll get in this lifetime.

"Nice one," my father says. He puts his own Callaway driver (brand new) back into his pro-style bag and steps into the driver's seat of the cart.

"Yeah," I say. "Finally got a good one."

Six years, as far as I can tell. Six years since I melted down in a local tournament and absolutely shit the bed, scored over 100 for the first time in forever crowned with a spectacular quintuple bogey, and told him I wouldn't be coming back. Six years since I was at this course, this country club in the middle of nowhere. It's almost my birthday and this is my birthday visit, and I don't know why I wanted to do this. Be back here with him, like nothing ever happened, welcomed back in spite of myself. Nothing ever that simple, though.

My father's drive is shorter than mine and landed in the rough, and I feel a little thrill of victory in spite of myself. First time I've picked up a club in a long time, and finally now, on the 18$^{th}$, I get a better drive than his off. I might be stronger but I haven't been playing, haven't been dedicating myself to the game the way he has. That's what golf takes, dedication, the mental ability to put the ball where you want it. I never had that.

We step off my father's ball, settled in the rough. Farthest from the flag goes first. His shot isn't great, the ball tangled in this Zosyia grass and with a piss poor approach. This won't be great. My father's been drinking but I've stuck with water, and the last few holes I've gotten steadily better while he's gotten worse, increasingly unsteady and frustrated. But he's happy I'm here, in his own limited way.

He's got a seven iron. On a par five like this (3 shots to reach the green, and two putts) this is a conservative play to say the least. On in three, staring down a birdie, maybe, but that's two long shots and like I said, he's getting unsteady.

The club twists in my father's hands and leaves him with a long approach to the green. I slide over to the driver's seat and let him into the other side. "Tough break."

"It was my fault," my father grunts. "I tried to do too much."

Oh, did he ever.

At my own ball I pull a three wood from my bag, my ancient and crusty, misused bag, and line up a perfect approach to the green. Just over water, easy as can be. More than enough club for a 180 yard shot. A cardinal sings in the middle of my backswing and I badly mishit the ball. It flies too low, too short, and lands in the exact center of the lake in front of the green.

Fuck. I drop another one, but it rolls into a much worse lie, leaving me less options.

"Move it," my father says. "We aren't in a tournament or anything."

I rinse this one, too.

"Sorry. You should have taken the drop closer, why didn't you?"

"I don't know," I say.

My father's next shot, a neat little 9 iron, winds up in the middle of the green.

I reach into my bag and pull another ball, then walk up to the edge of the lake and look into the water. This is a nice course by Abboton standards, but that doesn't mean this lake isn't more of a bog of shit than a body of water. Algae growing like a virus, and the whole thing has an unholy, insufferable stench. I breathe deep and take in a lungful. It smells like the Ohio. The water is dark and looks deeper than it is, and I can see a distorted reflection of myself in it. It would be too easy to fall in and stay in. I would drown if I could make myself stay underwater, but that isn't quite possible. I wonder if my father would pull me out, or even be able to. Maybe he'd just step on my head and make me go even faster. One time I dropped a brand new golf bag, this bag, in a water hazard that smelled just as foul as this one. My father yelled for hours, all the way back to the clubhouse. It would be fitting to meet my end like this.

"Hey. Hey. Are you going to take your shot?"

I snap out of it and take a few steps back. Stretch the arm out, perpendicular to the ground, and drop it. The ball lands in a good lie, for once. I pull a sand wedge out of the bag. I take a perfect swing, not too soft, but not too hard, and hit the ball right at its equator and it goes low again, skittering across the green and leaving me a long putt.

We both return to the cart. My father hits the gas pedal

and the electric motor hums smoothly, taking us around the water hazard and up to the green. "Hey, it's not so bad, right? Not like we're playing for money."

Well, he isn't. "Yeah."

On the green I line it up. I crouch behind his ball to read the curve of the green. It's a double-breaker, the final boss of golf shots: the ground curves once to the left, then once again to the right. I read it from the opposite side too. I go back behind the ball and dangle his putter between my thumb and first finger, like this is some kind of putt that matters, like I can make up for a missed career with this one shitty shot. I line it up and take a couple practice strokes.

Just as I take it away I realize, I haven't accounted for the putt being uphill, so I panic and put some extra juice behind it and smack the ball, ten feet past the hole.

My father lines up his own put and makes two confident practice strokes before lining up to his own ball. He looks at the hole and easily makes his putt. Birdie.

I miss the ten-footer too, and hole out for a ten on the hole. Quintuple bogey. The dreaded five over par.

We shake hands, joking. Again, nothing to be too formal about. No reason to make a big deal about it.

# CHAPTER 64

Instead of going back to their house, my house, where I belong and where we belong as a family, we eat in the dining room of the clubhouse. I can't help hating all of this, even though I should be grateful. I'm loaded up on Adderall again to get through this. Free meal and all that.

My mother, she hasn't seen me in a year. She meets us at the club and hugs me in her frail little arms, paper-white, translucent skin and dyed, thinning dirty blond hair. She's stressed and not taking care of herself, but it's none of my business so I won't say anything.

"It's so good to see you," she says. She gets a little teary. "You're so thin!"

Ham and bean soup, small talk, who's divorcing who, what's new in the neighborhood, Cesar salads, salmon, red wine, more and better food than I've had since I can remember. My father is terse, unwilling to talk, somewhere between performing a needed function and making some awkward attempt to connect.

"How's your job, Victor?" my mother asks me.

"Bad," I say. "That's it. Just bad."

"Oh." She's taken back and looks at my father, who is

picking at a crème brûlée, barely eating it. "So, what are you going to do about that?"

"I have a few ideas."

She looks at my father again but he's not saying anything, because we both know where this is going. Why else would I come to him, right? This is the ritual of the poor little rich boy, hat in hand, needing more money for drugs and rent.

"Suzanne! Haven't seen you in forever." Someone, one of my mother's friends is calling over to her from the bar. Ignoring my father, as usual.

"Oh hi Deborah! Tunde, it's Deborah," my mother says, and my father raises his spoon and half smirks. "I'm going to go over and say hi, I'll be right back."

She leaves us there, just my father and me. Darren's coming in a few days, to take a look at the store. To root out the thief. To fire me, or at least that was the original plan, before I told Britt what I needed her to believe.

"Dad?" I say.

"Yes, Victor?"

"I'm sorry."

He puts his spoon down and raises an eyebrow. "For what?"

"You know what."

"I really don't."

The bastard wants to draw it out of me, humiliate me, make me say it, detail my own crimes because he is an African father and African fathers are never wrong. They are perfect arbiters of truth and justice whose ways must not be questioned, and only condescend to acknowledge such errors as they deem necessary. But I won't do it, so at the very least I'll choose my own humiliation.

"I think I'm going to lose my job. And if not, I should probably quit anyway."

He shakes his head and drinks half his wine. "Unbelievable."

"There was a theft. Another theft. There are circumstances beyond my control. I'm not here asking for anything. I just want to make sure that our agreement still stands. I put my time in."

"That's all I am to you and your mother, aren't I? Just a wallet with legs. Nobody worried about what I want. Just take, take, take, all day."

"This isn't about that."

"I knew you were stealing from your store. Ever since you started hanging out with those alcoholics and drug dealers, I knew you would fall into the same pit. I was going to warn you of this when you moved, but I can see it didn't even take Manhattan to bring you to the wrong crowd."

I swallow. "How do you know any of my friends are dealers?"

He laughs, bitterly. Shakes his head, tongue clicking. "I can see it. I see many things, Victor. I just don't say anything."

"Will you stop? Please, just once listen to me. Just listen." I take a deep breath. "I'm moving. I'm moving out of town. I'm going to attend school, I'm going to get my degree and leave all of this behind me. And maybe, along the way, I'll come to you, and I'll beg you, tail between legs, for money, because I'm a fuck up and a loser and just a whole bundle of wasted potential. But I am not here for that. I am here because I would like to know that I still have a family."

He doesn't say anything, just pours himself more wine. The words don't settle with him. They barely settle with me. This kind of thing, it doesn't matter to people like us. Who cares if he hit me. This bastard is the only person I can trust in this world.

And one day I'll be just like him. I already talk to women the way he does, the way Henshaw does. Crown to brow, down the line. I put my head down and squint as hard as I can, white lights flashing big, holding in tears with all the muscles in my face.

"I'm not giving you money so you can continue your bad habits elsewhere."

"We can't change the past. We've both made mistakes, both done things we regret. You've done some things. Please. I need this."

"I've done nothing to you, Victor. Nothing to you or your mother. I know she tried to convince you, to turn you against me, but I've done nothing to you. I am getting older, and I cannot be expected to give away everything I have to someone who does not appreciate what I have to offer."

*My father lays his rifle across the bed and tells my mother "One of us is going to die tonight."*

"Your mother has convinced you that I'm a monster. That I am abusive. Was it abuse, caring for you all of these years? Was it abuse, clothing you, feeding you, working for you?"

"That wasn't it."

"Then what was? I gave you all this," and he waves his spoon again, at the walls, the ceiling, the overpaid, under-dressed membership and their bald spots. "You threw it away. You decided you would go hang out with your redneck white trash friends. That was your decision, not mine. I didn't want that for you. But what was I to do?"

"You threatened my mother with a gun."

"No, Victor. You don't understand, but one day you will. One day you will have a wife, and you will understand when she won't leave you alone. When she won't treat you with the respect you deserve. I look around and see how these women treat their husbands, worship the ground they walk on. Why can't I have that? You'll see one day. And then you'll under-stand what happened between my mother and me. When she screams at you after you have given her everything, you'll know. Your mother hasn't fucked me in three years. How do you think that feels? I don't want to get prostate cancer."

*My father lays his rifle across the bed and tells my mother "One of us is going to die tonight."*

"Are you telling me I imagined it?" I ask.

"I'm telling you that if you want my help, you should stop talking about this and start coming up with a plan for your own life." He spoons a little crème brûlée into his mouth. "Come back to me with a real plan, tell me exactly what you need, and we'll see. I'm willing to help, if you're willing to do the work. You're still young. You don't have to make my mistakes."

*My father lays his rifle across the bed and tells my mother "One of us is going to die tonight."*

*My mother puts the barrel to her head and says "Do it."*

"You're a fucking asshole," I say.

His eyebrow goes up. "That's fine. You can think that. I don't care. But look at you here, groveling to me for money because you can't take care of yourself. You know, I thought this would be different. I thought maybe you had come around, started to make the move towards where you need to be. But you're just here, being who you always were."

I put my head on the table and start crying, and I can't stop it.

"Are you crying? Victor. Stop crying right now. You are in public, stop crying."

I pick my head up and look him in the eye. "I'm a faggot. Did you know that? I sucked off one of my employees. I think he liked it, but it's hard to tell because of all the pills we were on."

"You need to think about your future and stop."

"I used to suck dick in college too. I'd go to the theater parties and get really hammered and blow guys in the bathroom because I was confused and ashamed, and of course I could never have a boyfriend or anything because you'd beat me for that too."

"No, you didn't." His voice is low but edged now.

"Oh I did, and it felt dirty and I liked it. And I do drugs too. I'm high right now. I sell drugs for Henshaw, because of all the debt I'm in. I drink constantly and get into fights and fuck random people, and sometimes I don't even use a condom. One time I let one of the caddies give me a blowjob in the locker room right over there."

"You're a disgrace."

I laugh, loud enough everyone can hear. "Hey y'all! Did you hear that? My father thinks I'm a disgrace because I like to suck dick."

"Victor."

"I'm 13 grand in debt. I don't even remember what I spent all the money on. But I'm guessing it was mostly pills."

"Victor, if you don't stop."

No one is looking at me, but that doesn't matter. I raise my voice. I'll make them listen.

"My name is Victor Adewale and I'm an alcoholic, a drug addict, and a bisexual party monster. And I regret none of it, because if the alternative was being an abusive Uncle Tom shithead like my father, I'm glad I chose to chemically fry my brain."

He stands up, red anger in his gaze.

"He threatened to kill my mother with a gun, more than once." I must admit, it feels good to have a stage. "Did you ever hear about that? But I'm the disaster because I sodomized a drag queen. I mean somebody fucking hang me, already."

I want to hit him, to beat him so badly he can't see. I want to spill his pretty red blood all over the tablecloth. My breathing goes shallow and I start rocking back and forth and the panic attack hits me and I start making a horrible sound, a keening screech that I'm trying to hold in. I get up and run outside and down the hill in the shallow evening light towards the putting green and then the screams come. I fall to my knees and grit my teeth to keep it in but I physically can't, I can barely breathe, and I keep screaming over and over, clutching my head, screaming like I did on the floor of my bedroom.

My mother comes up behind me. "What's wrong with you? Someone get help!"

"No," I manage to get out. "It'll pass."

But it keeps going, the screams muffled, my heart pounding deep in my chest, teeth grinding as I rock back and forth. Memories come flooding through, one after the other. The gun, the beatings, the screams, my mother being choked, my father's face an inch from mine, and below it all the undeniable fact that I have always needed him.

I vomit, all over the grass. Chunks of ham suspended in thin gruel of beer and stale alcohol. I lean back on my heels. They're both around me now. The workers and the other members on the patio, they're staring but pretending not to notice. Both of my parents have come to me now, my mother furious. My father, puzzled, like he's never seen anything quite like this.

# CHAPTER 65

The first day of Thunder Fest, I go alone. I have been ignoring my father's calls and voicemails and emails for a full 24 hours.

Henshaw is having a party tonight. He sent it out over mass text, inviting everyone he knows. I don't want to see him, but I'm also thinking it'll be great cover to get Kyle to come stay with me.

They shut down St. Joe, from MacArthur Memorial Park and two miles north, and pack the whole thing with food booths, one after the other, on both sides of the street. The park itself and the adjoining street are packed with shitty carnival rides that smell of grease and age, with terrible tinny speakers and booming dubstep roaring out at every angle.

The real attraction is those food booths though. Giant corn dogs, ribeye sandwiches, elephant ears (big flapping sheets of fried dough covered in sugar), lemon shake-ups, stromboli (but not the right kind they sell you in back east, no this is a sub filled with pizza toppings), funnel cakes, Scotch eggs, gyros, whole potatoes cut into ribbons and fried, shish kabobs, pork tenderloin (the national sandwich of Indiana, a piece of pork pounded flat the size of a vinyl record, breaded and deep-fried and served on a laughably minuscule bun), and the absolute crown jewel of the whole thing, the fried cow brain sandwich, sold at a single one of 150 booths. I've never eaten one.

Abboton is the fattest city in America.

I pitch my head back and yell "Whoop, whoop," with lots of bass and an upward inflection, and sure enough I hear it repeated back to me, faintly from some other corner of the vast labyrinth of carts. The call of the Juggalo. They love Thunder Fest. I know for a fact that Lex is here, and he will be here all day every day, damn near open to close. I think about trying to find him but decide not to, unless it just happens that way.

Oh, you can drink on the street during Thunder Fest, too. I duck into this country bar, and get an aluminum bottle Bud Light. I shouldn't be drinking. I've been feeling unstable, and unhinged, and I am wretchedly, incorrigibly, incurably, inexplicably sad, and the alcohol is not helping.

If I stay here all night I'll start seeing people I know, people from shows and college and jobs I used to work. I know this from coming here with Lex, time and time again, year after year, the two of us fighting the crowds and taking breaks for beer and watching baseball games in the German bar/restaurant on Franklin. Henshaw hates to go, the rat fuck, so I've always been Lex's running buddy for this thing. I don't mind it, all things considered. It kills time and it's relaxing, the two primary pastimes of the people of Abboton.

They're square dancing on the big stage halfway down the street, set up with lights and sounds. They hold contests and recitals there all week, lame-ass standard boring old-fashioned Hoosier shit, things that reflect the over-30 crowd and entertain the country folk from out of town but don't remotely interest any of us, the mean and young and empty.

I buy a Scotch egg as a kind of deference to expectation. It's a hard-boiled egg wrapped in sausage then rolled in breadcrumbs and deep fried. My dad used to make them before he stopped cooking, because Nigeria is a British colony and they spread that way, probably from India where they stuff meatballs with eggs. My father's are spicier and more tender. These are too crispy and coarse, and there's too much sage, but I scarf it down anyway with sips of beer because it kind of does remind me of home. It's my favorite thing to get here, the only thing I get every year.

The rides and game section smells like it ought, absolutely foul. Isn't it beautiful, though? Almost everyone comes here for the food and camaraderie, to see people they haven't seen in a while, to celebrate nothing at all but also to celebrate being alive in some kind of minor way. At least that's why I'm here.

"Yo, Vic!"

It's Lex, with his teenage sister Becky and an older couple in tow. I knew I'd find him.

"Yeah man, are you good though?" he asks.

"Yeah," I lie. I smile at his sister and look pointedly at the couple.

"Oh yeah, this is my moms, and her husband. This my friend Vic, guys. This kid is the man, ya heard?"

I shake their hands. Both are tall. The mother has an exceedingly kind but busted-up face, not that old but worn down from years of what I assume is smoking. The dad's got a white ponytail and a mustache and a kind of smirk, and he's eating a corndog that he moves to the other hand while he shakes my hand.

"Pleasure to meet you," I say, to each in turn.

"You boys hang out a lot, then?" his mom asks.

"You know it," I say.

"Well good, that's lovely. Alexander is a good kid."

"He really is."

"Kevin," Becky says "I wanna ride the Ferris wheel. You got the ticket."

"Hold on a second," he says. "Let me finish this first, then we'll go."

Just a regular family like everyone else. We're all

thrashing crazy drunks with bad attitudes, troublesome kids, but somebody loves us. Some approximation of a family, be it a substitute or a step-parent or a lover. No one escapes humanity. How hard it must be to be a real monster.

"Hey Lex," I say. "I'm gonna walk around, alright? Find a beer, maybe a turkey leg or something."

"I'll find you," he says. "Oh yeah, you coming to Henshaw's party tonight?"

Night falls as we walk around, telling ancient jokes and running into old faces, clusters of kids sitting on ledges where they don't belong, guys that just got out of lockup, passing cart after cart, the smells growing in intensity while announcers remind everyone through massive speakers where lost and found is, and what act is next up on the main stage. I try to drink it all in, all of it, every last bit of it, every neon light and whiff of pop country, every face, the location of the peeking stars, the way the air sits just a little too heavy on shoulders, the lingering stink of the Ohio.

# CHAPTER 66

*We need to talk about your finances,* my father texts me. *After your little stunt this past week, I can no longer be attached to you like this. You have obviously taken a path I do not approve of, and I must think of what is best for my family. I have a reputation and a life that I have built for myself, and I cannot allow you to mortgage that. It is time for you to build your own. There must be a separation.*

K, I text back, 4 hours later.

# CHAPTER 67

Two bottles on Henshaw's kitchen counter stand out to me out of the half-gallons of vodka and the beer: Everclear and Hpnotiq. I tell Amory to wait as I pull two knockoff red Solo cups from their plastic sheathe and fill them with ice.

"Alright, you need to try this, okay?"

"Okay," she says. "I trust you."

*1 part Everclear*

*1 ½ parts Hpnotiq*

*3 parts Sprite*

*Pour Everclear and Hpnotiq over ice. Fill with Sprite.*

She takes a sip and screws her face up, before letting it relax, surprised. "That's not terrible. I saw the Everclear and I was scared, but it's not bad."

"Right? It's drinkable. I call it a Blue Disaster."

"You make that up?"

"Yup. Cheers," I say, and we clink glasses, or more like squish since they're plastic.

The place is packed and I don't see Henshaw, which you know, thank fuck. I don't see Kyle either. I haven't spoken to him since we hooked up, and neither has Amory. We considered waiting for him to leave work, but that would just freak him out.

I try to make small talk with some random people. It's a lot of standing around nodding going "Uh huh, no way, fuck off," ad nauseum. It's tiring, and once I let slip that I work at Redacted everyone wants to ask me questions, see if they can find out what's coming in, what it's like working there.

"Can you get me your discount?" some guy asks me. I try not to stare at his lazy eye but it's not easy.

"Nah man, sorry," I say.

Amory slides off to the back to maybe use the restroom but I think she's actually trying to get a burger from Lex. I escape to the front porch. It's not dark yet, still burnt blue twilight, and people are still filtering in and out from the festival. There's the intermittent pop and bang of firecrackers, or what could be gunshots. It's not strictly illegal to blow off fireworks on days that aren't the 4th, but it is frowned upon. Still, it's ThunderFest, so the cops are somewhat more lenient when it comes to noise. I'm feeling pretty chill and almost forgetting myself when I see Erica's car, sliding across the street into the space between two Hondas, someone I can't see well enough to recognize in the passenger seat. She parallel parks, carefully but not carefully enough, too close on the back side of the car. The doors open and Erica steps out, blue-ass hair longer than before, roots showing and drawn back into the usual ponytail, bobbing in the light wind. And out of the backseat tumbles Kyle.

Henshaw comes up behind me. "Hey. Didn't see you come in."

"I've been here. Why is Kyle with Erica?"

"Had her pick him up from work. Am I allowed to do that?"

"Didn't say you weren't." I take a sip. "You alright man?"

"It's Thunder Fest! Which apparently matters," and he holds up his hand for a weak high-five.

I watch Kyle and Erica stumble their way into the house.

Kyle is holding a Redacted bag. I want to look inside but I'm interrupted by Lex crashing his way up towards us, giving us both big hugs.

"All my favorite people," he says. "Hey just so you know, we're out of hamburger buns."

Henshaw jerks his head towards me. "Vic can go."

An idea comes to me. "Sure, I can go. Kyle, wanna come with?"

He looks at Henshaw, frightened, and shakes his head.

"I'll go," says Erica.

"Just head to the CVS," Henshaw says. "They should have them there. Shouldn't be too long."

I can see Amory behind him, talking to somebody, arms crossed. "Tell Amory I'll be right back, okay?"

"Amory," Henshaw says.

The inside of my car smells like old tacos and ash. Erica rolls the window down as I pull away from the curb.

"I don't think I've ever ridden in your car," she says. "It's nice. So. Amory," Erica says.

"What about her?"

"Do I know her?"

"She's met the guys but no, I don't think y'all have met. I went to college with her."

"College girl."

CVS is far from packed, most people having already done their last-minute shopping and moved onto their respective parties and cookouts. Erica and I weave our way through, grabbing both hot dog and hamburger buns, more Sprite, potato chips.

"You and Henshaw a thing again?" I ask.

"No. Besides, that's none of y'all's business."

I think I recognize the cashier, a short stocky kid I ran into at a show once, but don't ask since I don't feel like talking. We pile into my car awkwardly, shoving the shit in the back seat without much care, not concerned with the bread or any of it. I take the long way back to the place.

"Look, I just don't want any trouble." I say.

"I'm not giving you trouble. You can do whatever you want with your college girl. I'll just be sitting here, waiting for you like always."

"You aren't waiting for me."

"You only called me when you wanted to get laid. You don't bring me to your place, and you never buy me anything even though I've bought you and your friends food all the time. I get that I'm just your fuck doll. But don't expect me to be happy about it."

"You texted me last time. You used me. Just don't start shit, alright? All I'm asking."

"Fine."

# CHAPTER 68

It's late. Real alcoholic late, end of the party late. Me, Henshaw, Lex, Erica, Kyle, and Amory are the only ones left. Spotify on shuffle, first Odd Future then Katy Perry then Fall Out Boy, real trash music, total mall shit. I've lost track of how many drinks I've had but everything is sliding and it's getting harder to hear. Great billowing clouds drifting over the wreckage of the party, the paper waste of hundreds of fireworks and the typical red cups, blue and white powder residue on a Slipknot CD case.

Amory and I sit on the porch, leaning against the house's siding. She's the only one that isn't drunk, not really. Kyle sits at our feet, obviously wasted, pilled out, barely able to stay sort of vertical.

"You need help," Amory says. "I didn't know it was this bad."

"How did you not?" I say. "Like no offense, but you're friends."

"I don't have any friends," he says.

She holds him close. "We're your friends Kyle. Henshaw is not your friend. We can help you." She looks up at me, like I'm supposed to be the savior.

"Yeah, I want to," I say. "Except, oh yeah, you tried to frame me."

"Don't be an asshole. We can help you, I promise. You just need to let us. If you go to a facility they can help you. They might not even prosecute."

"Oh, they'll prosecute," he says. His voice breaks in sobs. "Nothing good happens to people like me. Just one fucked up thing after another."

We pick him up and try to lay him down on the couch, but Henshaw and Erica are sitting there, cuddled together. Kyle shrugs us off and goes into his room. My fury is growing by leaps and bounds, too much for me to maintain, too much for me to deal with even as I try to keep it together. I am better than this, I am the adult, the one who is in control. This is my life and I must take control, even if my future is predetermined.

Kyle comes back with the Redacted bag and drops it in Henshaw's lap before returning, wordlessly, to his room. Henshaw opens the bag and pulls out stacks of bills one after the other, thousands of dollars rubber-banded together.

"Thanks, man" he says. "Been waiting on this."

"That's from my store, Henshaw," I say. "You can't just take the money he stole from my store."

"And why not? Are you going to pay my mortgage, cake eater? Or do you have some other solution. You keep picking up this scum, first this fag and then that absolute trash dyke you've been fucking. I don't blame you though, like she's hot. Hotter than Erica."

"Excuse me?" Erica says. She pushes against him to stand but he tightens his grip on her.

"I mean, it's true. That's the advantage I have over you, cake eater. I can see reality and I'm not afraid to speak my mind."

I move towards the bag and he clutches it, holding it out of my grasp.

"Oh now, don't do something you'll regret, cake eater. Go home and fuck your dyke. That's what I'm about to do."

Amory pokes her head in, a bland look on her face. "Just so you know, I can hear you."

Erica tears up and runs down the hall into the bathroom. Henshaw gets up and goes into Kyle's room, shutting the door behind him.

"Let me drive us home, okay?"Amory says.

I nod and press my car keys into her hand and we walk up the block back to my car. When we get there my conscience starts to burn and I realize that I can't leave Kyle alone with Henshaw, that I don't trust something to not go down between them. Wordlessly I turn and go back to the house, pushing the unlocked, ajar door open, and then I see something.

Henshaw has Kyle pinned up against the wall, face first, fresh bruises on his cheeks and blood running down his nostril mixing with tears. His pants are pulled down to his knees and Henshaw is fucking him, hard, enough that there's a trickle of blood running down Kyle's leg. His eyes turn and meet mine and I can see him pleading towards me.

Kyle's been raped before. He'd told me about the incident in the frat house when we were both in college when he got too stoned to move. But I don't think this is something that gets easier, and I suddenly realize it's not the first time he's had Henshaw's dick in him.

Henshaw turns to me. "What do you want, faggot?" He's still pumping away. "You trying to get in on this?"

I step away, my hands in the air. The full scope of their relationship is coming into focus andI don't want to be involved. Henshaw can keep Kyle for all I care.

But something in me enrages Henshaw. He pulls out and makes a move as I back away and suddenly he's all over me, elbow in my face, knees on my stomach. I flail my arm out and connect with something but it doesn't matter, he's already on my throat, pinning me to the wall. There's no pain. Just rage, that blinding, all-consuming and all-satisfying and righteous desire to hurt someone that I haven't felt in so long, tamped down for years. I keep flailing, unwilling to let it go as my ears fill with a roaring I don't know. I'm finding new kinds of rage as this seems to go on forever and ever, just building up with no release like the mosh pit except it's worse this time because I'm losing. I know I'm hurting even if the pain isn't there yet. He manages to get me down onto the ground and goddamn, Henshaw is a big mother fucker, huge bones, knots of muscle and a thick layer of fat all pressing down on me to no end filling up my whole world until there's nothing but his shirt and the inconceivable mass bearing down on me. The big meat wall finally comes down on me.

He grabs me by my bare skull and forces my head upwards. I feel the dick in my mouth before I see it, in fact I can't see anything out of my right eye. He fucks my mouth with a violence that tells me he's not getting any pleasure out of this. The taste is sour and reminds me of balsamic vinegar, and I can smell sweat and shit. I flail around, hitting as much of him as I can, but I might as well be slapping the side of a barn.

"You like that?" he says. "You like that white boy dick, you fucking nigger. Suck it. Bite and I'll kill you both."

He comes down my throat and I start choking. I hear Kyle screaming for him to get off me. Suddenly the pressure relieves and I hear more blows land, then the sick sound of breaking glass. My right eye hurts, and there's coppery wet on my face. I look over and Henshaw stands over the remains of the table. Kyle's at his feet, bleeding from the head and moaning softly in pain.

For a moment, no one says anything. Henshaw turns and walks past me, dick still out, as if he's in a daze. I roll over to feel Kyle's pulse, glass cutting into my flesh. He's alive for sure. I rip off part of his shirt and try to staunch the bleeding from his head. I say his name but he's too out of it to respond to me.

From behind me comes the sound of a pistol slide. I turn my head to see Henshaw, pointing his handgun at me. And now I see him. Eyes that tell me he's killed before, eyes that are willing to kill me now, and he'd probably get away with it.

"Get the fuck out of my house," he says. The calm in his voice, more deadly than any beating. "If I see either of you again, I'll kill you."

This is his response. Not to call 911, not to express any shred of human kindness. I pick up Kyle. There's blood all over me. I get him out, half dragging him across the lawn towards my car. Henshaw slams the door behind us. I yell back at the house.

"You better fucking kill me next time. Do you hear me?" My voice is already giving out. "I swear on my fucking soul, if you ever touch me again. You better fucking kill me."

Amory gets out of the driver's seat and helps me get Kyle in the backseat. She drives. The city is coming awake and the air is chilly. There's dew everywhere, and too many cars on the road. Long lines at McDonald's for breakfast. I hold Kyle's hand. My vision isn't right. Half of everything is blurry, incomprehensible. There's plenty of blood on the seats, and I groan.

"You're fucking up the leather, man."

"Really?" Amory asks in disgust.

Then in the smallest voice, Kyle grumbles. "Pleather."

My father used to say, *The dog that does not hear the call of its master is a lost dog.*

What a fucking disappointment.

# CHAPTER 69

We sit together in the emergency room, Amory and I. I put her on the left, since the right side of my vision has gone black. We've been here for hours, waiting to hear a prognosis. There wasn't any wait, and I'm guessing given the nature of Kyle's injury there wouldn't be much of one anyway.

"Do you think he'll be alright?" I ask. I can still taste bitter skin in my mouth.

"What happened, Victor?" she asks me in response.

I assumed, in my selfishness, that the nature of me and Amory's relationship is what would rest most heavily on me. But instead I'm genuinely concerned for Kyle. I'm not in love or anything, but somehow the idea of losing him terrifies me. And it's clear that Amory knows this. Then again, I suppose polyamory wouldn't be out of the question.

The nurse comes out to speak to us. We exchange names.

"He's awake," she says. "But out of it. You can come see him, if you want."

His head is heavily bandaged. The heart monitor beeps. His eyes are open, but they stare blankly towards the ceiling, no expression on his face at all. I've never been in a hospital room like this. I'm sobering up too, which isn't fun. This

moment crossfades with all the times I've seen this on televi-
sion, and reality slips. I reach out to hold Amory's hand, and
to my surprise she lets me.

"Hey, Kyle," I say. "How's it hanging?"

He doesn't answer me, or make any sign that he recognizes us or heard anything at all. I reach out and touch his
hand, to connect all of us. He makes no motion, positive or
negative.

"He's catatonic," the nurse says. "The doctor says he's
concussed, but beyond that we're unsure what's wrong. It
could be psychological. We're running pharmacology tests as
well."

I know what's wrong, but I don't bother filling them in.

Do you have any contact info for the family?" the nurse
asks.

"No," we say.

"Do you know where he lives?"

"He can't go back there," Amory says through a sob.

"Oh." The nurse is quiet for a moment. "Can you tell us
what happened again?"

"He fell down some stairs," Amory says.

"My best friend tried to kill us," I say.

The nurse looks up from her clipboard, nonplussed. "So
which is it?"

"Do you have anyone around who can take a look at my
eye? I can't see shit."

The nurse excuses herself, no doubt to find a police officer. I just stare at Kyle's face. Even in silence, he doesn't seem
at peace.

# AUGUST

# CHAPTER 70

They put a patch over my right eye last night. The doctor said it was a retinal detachment, and that they were unsure if I would see again. I already know the answer, but I thought it would be funnier if I didn't tell them. My lip is regular swollen, not badly swollen. I show up to work late, inhumanly calm.

"What happened to you?"

I smile, and my upper lip starts bleeding again. "Fell down some stairs." A couple approaches the door and I turn to them, still smiling. "Hey guys, how are you doing? Anything I can help you find? Okay, well let me know, shirts are buy one, get one half off."

They scuttle away, clutching each other.

"Just so you know," Britt says, "There were these two black guys and this fat black girl in here earlier, looking suspicious, fingering merchandise, you know." She rearranges the hot pink coolers. Her eyes are red from crying, and I realize that today isn't going to be good for her either. "How does it make you feel, that half your race makes the other half look bad?"

I look at her, too hurt to feel it. "They don't."

"By the way, speaking of theft."

"Yes?"

"Darren's in the back. Came by early. There's a cop back there too. They need to talk to you."

I go in the back and find Darren sitting there, legs crossed at that one table, another chair pulled out for me. His ThinkPad is sitting in front of, him open to Outlook. He stands to greet me. Tall, imposing fucker. But he shrinks back at the sight of my face.

"Good lord, Vic. What happened to you?"

"I don't know what you're talking about. Shall we begin?"

I hold out my hand and Darren, at a loss, gives it a shake. Powell leans up against the wall. He doesn't shake my hand.

"I'm sure you must be confused," Darren begins.

How am I any different from these people? In every meaningful way, I am a Hoosier. I swim in the Ohio in spirit if not body. My feet are rooted in the concrete and my breath swims through the parking lots and trees and between the smokestacks. These eyes are filled with orange sodium light. I can see the flashes in the corner of my bad eye. The smell, the look, *the fuck it* attitude and backstabbing, the petty trading of sexual partners and favors, the expectation that nothing is ever going to be better than it is right here and now. I am an Abbtonian.

"Well," I say. "Wouldn't be the first time I've spoken to an officer in here."

Powell gives a dry chuckle and Darren frowns.

"You know why I was coming down here originally. It's an LP thing, trying to figure out why your shrink was up and really get to the bottom of that. So I'm just going to go ahead and ask you some questions anyway, just to get this out of the way." Darren clears his throat. "So your store does more than anticipated volume considering the size of your market, and similar stores in the district. Why do you think this is?"

"Well," I say, "I think it's because we cater to a very specific clientele, and I think that there is a higher concentration of this clientele than there might be other places such as Indianapolis or Bloomington."

He's puzzled. That's the wrong answer, and managers always give the right answer. "Can you elaborate?"

"Sure. Abboton is kind of stuck in the 90s, so it makes sense that a store which sells a lot of outdated stuff like cartoon t-shirts would do well."

"So you don't ascribe any of this to Britt's leadership."

"Britt is an incredibly hard worker who deserves to be paid a lot more than she is. But no."

"Would you describe store morale as good?"

"I would describe it mostly as low-key suicidal."

Darren sighs and puts down his pen. "Is something wrong, Vic?"

"I can take it from here," Powell says. He pulls out the third metal folding chair and takes a seat caddy corner to us. "I don't know if you're aware, but this store was hit again. Last night."

"That's terrible news."

"You were mentioned in a police report last night." Powell doesn't need any paper to intimidate me. He just keeps his arms crossed. "Or should I say, early this morning. It involved you, and one of your associates, and his roommate. Is there any connection between that and this robbery?"

"Not that I'm aware of."

"But you have to admit it's odd." He leans forward in his chair. "I mean, both of you work here, and all of a sudden his roommate snaps and you both get beat up?"

"My friends are very spirited."

Darren cuts across him. "Vic, we're trying to help you here. We're trying to help the whole store."

"There is no connection," I say.

"Who took the money, Vic?"

"I don't know."

Powell laughs, for a long time. "Did you not investigate this?"

"I was told not to. By Britt."

"Why is that?"

"Because it's not my responsibility to investigate this."

"I could have you in cuffs right now. Do you realize that? There's enough here for me to bring you down to the station and book you. And if there isn't, I'm sure I could figure it out. I want to know everything you know about this. No more stonewalling, no more bullshit. Tell us now."

I look at him. I am unafraid, because I finally know what it means to have nothing to lose.

"I don't know anything about this," I say. "And if I did, I certainly wouldn't be talking to you without a lawyer."

Powell sighs. Leans back in his chair. "Where's Kyle?"

"Catatonic down at Gateway."

"Maybe I'll go talk to him. Might be more helpful. You can go."

I shake both their hands and leave the back room. I clock out at the computer and walk back towards the Plate. Patrick and Sandy are standing around, pale and scared, watching me. I don't say anything to them, not even a nod. There's nothing left to say.

"Hey," Britt calls at me. "Pocket Check."

I look down. I've already crossed the threshold. But I come back and do the whole thing for her, turn out my pockets, show off my socks.

"I know it was Kyle," she says.

I don't say anything. Just put my stuff back in my pockets.

Ten thousand dollars is a lot of money to just go missing under your watch.

"I thought it was you," she says.

I look at her through my one good eye. "I know."

# CHAPTER 71

I am 8 years old.

"Grip the club in your fingers. Now link your right pinky and your left pointer together. No, like this." My father puts down his club and places his black hands with their worn pink palms upon my small brown ones, and wraps my hands around the black and green grip of his old pitching wedge.

"Good. Now address the ball." He places a single golf ball out of the massive bucket we're sharing on the green Astro-Turf mat and steps back to my right side onto the concrete. "Bend at the hips. Now, bend your knees. You want to be flexible. Relax. Don't be so tense. Now look where you want it to go."

I look out onto the lighted range and see several flags. Around us balls fly out of stalls at varying heights and curvatures. I pick the nearest flag.

"Now swing with your body."

I take the club back as far as I can and swing it through. I make decent contact and the ball flies about 30 yards.

"There you go. Good job." He puts another ball on the mat. "Try it again."

# CHAPTER 72

I let Amory smoke in my apartment. It's not like I don't do it all the time. She came here so I could fill her in on the rest of what happened that night.

"You must have done a hell of a job ratting Kyle out." She goes to light her cigarette, then stops when she sees the look on my face. "Kidding."

She motions for me to sit next to her and I do, my junk uncomfortably swinging in my shorts.

"I wanted to get away from this," she says. "I got a scholarship and took out loans and went to college. And yet here I am."

I stare at the TV. Dead and black, an old cathode ray tube because I'm too broke to afford even a Craigslist one.

She's crying now, not much, but enough. "If I see Henshaw again, I'll fucking kill him myself. I wish I'd taken Kyle in. None of this would have happened."

"Henshaw's right, you know. I am a brat. Lucky."

"Dude, who cares. Fuck Henshaw."

Every day I check the paper to see if either of them have been arrested. It would bring me equal relief and pain to see Kyle's mugshot. They let Sandy keep her job, but the rest of us are out by the end of the month. I called Britt, but only got her voicemail.

"Hopefully he'll plea. I don't want to testify. Assuming they don't arrest me first."

She leans into me. "They won't."

"Why are you still here?"

"Because I don't have anyone else to share this with, and I don't want to be alone."

"That's sad."

"It's exactly as sad as every other relationship."

# CHAPTER 73

I wake up in the middle of the night and roll off the mattress onto the floor. Amory is still sleeping next to me, and I'm trying not to wake her up so I don't search for pants even though I'm naked. I go to the bathroom and pee in the dark, trying to aim for the edge of the bowl so I don't make too much noise. When I'm done I don't flush and wash my hands in the thinnest stream of water I can manage.

I look outside the front window of the living room at the parking lot below, the multicolored sea of cars rendered almost the same color by the streetlights. All of it, quiet. All I've ever known. Everything made smooth and uniform and low-key, evened out for the sake of convenience.

When I get back into bed Amory shifts and groans. Her eyes are open. I lay on my side and face her as she pulls the blanket up under her chin.

# CHAPTER 74

There is one last party at Lex's. We attend, even though we shouldn't. There's a nice finality to the way he shakes my hand. We will never be friends again, but at least we could do it face-to-face.

"I don't want to leave you behind," Amory says. We share a cigarette on the porch again.

"I can't stay here," I say. "That's for sure."

It's so beautiful out tonight. I can hear the mechanical rhythm of the city inside me, syncing up with the party noises, the crickets and the lightning bugs. For a moment we live to the same beat, spaced out and stretched forever to infinite space. Words go on forever, and I can reach my long clean limbs out into the night air and feel them go on forever too.

"If you treat me like you treated Erica, or even Kyle," Amory says. "I won't let you stay."

The weight of my sins rests in me like a puck of hardness, making every breath difficult. It will stay there for years, reminding me of what I am, never letting me forget. I wonder if everyone carries something like this, a dark splotch of gravity that tells them they are capable of evil. But then I remember the magnificent lightness as well. I have shared it with Amory some nights, and with Lex and Erica and even Henshaw. It is a spaciousness and purity on a hot clear summer night, when everyone is laughing and nothing hurts, and all you will ever need is each other. We are each the villain of someone else's story, no matter how much we are loved.

"I believe you," I say.

There is a commotion in the house, but my ears are so filled with something else I can't make out what it is, a tussle or something joyous. I can't tell who's involved or what's going on, and under the sodium lights everything is orange, both clear and blurry. The noise is getting louder now, roaring out the back too, coming around through the spaces between the houses. It builds, until finally it comes loose and a wave of humanity, more people than I thought could possibly be at this party come running out. They look like Henshaw and Lex and Patrick and Erica, and even Britt, countless faces and bodies seemingly smashed together. They roll out onto the lawn, roaring with the sound of humanity, smelling of liquor. Now the neighbors are on their porches, and people on bikes have hopped off to join the endless throng in the street. They gyrate to some unknown force, gnashing teeth and pressing flesh, the great booming in and out of the city their music, driving them in and out, to and fro, gloriously and horribly free of all restraint. And it spreads down the block, people appearing from within gardens and houses all moving the same way, the city come alive. There is no winner, just the bruises and scars left and that wonderful feeling that I am no longer a part of. I am too afraid to join, and then I realize Amory isn't standing either. She sits unmoved, tingling with the energy but stock still. So we sit there all through the night as the whole city comes alive like never before, two figures apart, side by side.

# ACKNOWLEDGMENTS

I would like to thank Christoph and Leza for taking a chance on this thing and shepherding it through from manuscript to book.

Enormous thanks to David Lipsky for his invaluable lessons and edits, Darin Strauss for his knowledge, Rick Moody for his toughness, and Joyce Carol Oates for her encouragement.

I would also like to thank my friends from Evansville, IN for being in my life, for better or worse, and my professors Carole Chapman and Margaret McMullan for their support in my early days of fumbling authorship.

I must thank my cohort at NYU for their feedback, and specifically Joanna Margaret for her endless patience, as well as Robin Whitely for his friendship and Conor Kelley for reaching out to me just as I hit bottom.

My dear friend Astro Pittman kept me going at some of my darkest times when I thought this novel would never exist, as did Ashley McQuown, Jesse Nicholson, Alix Melton, and William Johnson.

My buddy Manuel Marrero printed my stories at a time when I believed no one would, as did Heath Ision, William Druyea, and Rudy Johnson. Big thanks to Mellinda Hensley for giving me a push when I thought I had laid down my pen for good.

Thanks to my previous publishers, Philip Best and Evan Femino.

And of course, my thanks to my mother for fostering my love of reading and writing and to my father, the bastard.

# ABOUT THE AUTHOR

Alexandrine Ogundimu is an author. She reps both New Jersey and Indiana. She received her MFA at NYU and has been nominated for a Pushcart. She lives in New York City.

# ALSO BY CLASH BOOKS

PROXIMITY
Sam Heaps

DARRYL
Jackie Ess

GAG REFLEX
Elle Nash

HEXIS
Charlene Elsby

LIFE OF THE PARTY
Tea Hacic-Vlahovic

MARGINALIA
Juno Morrow

THE PAIN EATER
Kyle Muntz

I'M FROM NOWHERE
Lindsay Lerman

DARK MOONS RISING ON A STARLESS NIGHT
Mame Diene

WE PUT THE LIT IN LITERARY

clashbooks.com

FOLLOW US

Twitter

IG

FB

@clashbooks